BREATHLESS CITY

RENÉE DES LAURIERS

For Maya

Stella took her pill and felt it activate—sliding down her trachea like a rough gasp of air and working its way into her lungs. There, for the next ten hours, the little pill would coordinate oxygen exchange. The pressure in her nose and mouth numbed, shutting down, cutting off her need to breathe completely. Protecting her from the toxins in the air. Stella always took pills when others were watching—especially here, underground in the tunnels.

She was breathless.

Her contact was late, which was odd. For weeks, he'd left signal flags outside the city entrance requesting a meeting. Now there was less than three full hours of daylight left. She'd spent too much time underground already.

Her fingers trembled, and she clenched her hands into fists to stop the shaking. *Don't show these people any weakness.*

She'd wait fifteen minutes more. If she rushed and didn't run into trouble, it would be enough time.

A maintenance crew worker stopped short at the sight of Stella. Or, rather, at the sight of the interlocking blades tattooed on her pale skin. The ink design on her upper arm marked her as an outsider. Her albino coloring exposed her as the Ghost of Metzger's gang. The worker turned and rushed back the way he came.

The tunnels of the underground city were constructed from a hasty mismatch of available metals. The walls were painted in the nicer areas of the city. Here, they were not. Portions of the wall were marred with gashes in the five-line pattern of human fingernails. There were more scratches and stains close to the stairs leading to the outside world— close to where they kept the dialysis machines.

The squelch of sneakers against linoleum announced the nurse. He swept a hand across his forehead, wiping away sweat, and gave Stella a jerky nod, gesturing for her to follow.

Even in the private transfusion room, shut off from prying eyes, the nurse spoke in low tones, as if afraid someone would overhear their conversation via the narrow door gap. He was paranoid as always. It wasn't as if people could hear them through concrete and steel walls.

"I pulled together what I could," the nurse muttered. "We had an outbreak. Medical supplies are under new restrictions."

Laid out on the table were a drawstring pouch and a factory issued bottle. Starting with the pouch, Stella removed a handful of pills, inspecting them. Close up, the mechanisms on the outer shell resembled spinning clock gears. Real pills were far heavier than their small size suggested. Stella checked the number stamp. These were tens and twenty-fours. Which was all right. She'd prefer to see some forty-eights or more, but she hadn't come for oxygen pills.

She picked up the bottle and heard the clink of the sole antibiotic tablet rattle around inside.

Stella closed her eyes, gritting her teeth. "Don't bother to signal me if you're just going to waste my time."

Medical supplies were sometimes available in abandoned stores and the odd overlooked cabinet—but they were getting rarer. There was no guarantee she'd find antibiotics. At any rate, she wouldn't have much time to search until tomorrow. If Natalia could last that long.

Returning the pills, Stella shook her head. She'd loop around to the partially flooded CVS on her way back. That one still had products boxed away in the back. If it was unoccupied. Or if she could create enough of a distraction to get in.

"You haven't been around in a month. It's not like I can keep this on hand for you," the nurse hissed. "That antibiotic isn't scavenge quality. It came straight from the factory. One of them will make a difference. I can get more in a few days."

One antibiotic tablet, even straight from the factory, wasn't enough. Stella headed back out the door.

"Wait, where are you going?" the nurse asked.

Stella ignored him. She was halfway to the first turn in the tunnel when the nurse caught up.

"I can offer you more," he said in a low voice.

"Medical supplies?"

"Better." He held up a plain brass key.

"What's that?" Stella snapped.

"The only key that matters."

The key to shipments?

Supplies weren't accessible to just anyone. The path was locked at multiple stop points. With that key, she'd have direct access to the food, medicine and pills. Straight from the factory.

Problem was, the locks were also heavily guarded, deep

in the center of the city. Much farther than was safe for her. Did he think she was stupid enough to go into the heart of the underground?

Was it even real? Advance guards and administrators had sets. It would be difficult for the nurse to get his hands on one, but not impossible. The only clue to authenticity was his tight grip on the metal.

"That doesn't help me now." She was wasting time talking to him.

"I can pull in favors. I'll have more tomorrow."

One capsule of antibiotics. It wasn't enough. But it was all she could guarantee for Natalia. For now.

"Fine." Stella returned to the transfusion room to make the trade.

She pulled up her sleeve. The crook of her elbow was riddled with tiny marks and scars surrounding raised and darkened veins.

The nurse eased a cannula needle into the soft skin of her arm. Her blood flowed through a tube, dripping steadily into an IV bag.

Nausea pooled in the pit of her stomach. Her heart thudded loud enough for her to hear it in her ear. Stella dug her fingernails into the table to keep herself grounded as the room spun. It was less than ten percent of her blood volume, well within the acceptable range of blood loss. Her body should have been able to handle it.

Within her, the oxygen pill ticked faster, picking up the strain. *I can't keep doing this.*

Needle withdrawn, Stella lowered her sleeve. Trade complete.

～

STELLA FOLLOWED THE TRAIL OF LIGHT STREAKS REFLECTED from overhead bulbs. She was surrounded by the machines. The medical tunnels were impossible to avoid, as most of them were stationed near the exit of the city. Each was filled with patients on dialysis machines.

Bloodlines carried brown-tinged and blackened blood from the veins of strapped down patients. Pulsing mechanically, blood was pulled into machines that filtered out the toxins. The persistent beeping was too much like a robotic heartbeat.

Stella avoided eye contact with the patients. Some were just weakened, while others had skin necrosis or amputations. Rows of patients filled both sides of the tunnel. All of that sickness and disease seemed to close in on her. Time seemed to stretch out in front of her as she counted out the steps that would take her home.

Be invisible.

Most people recognized the tattoo of Xander Metzger's gang and avoided her. Even here, in the hospital wing, the medical staff scuttling about would step out of her way. But Stella heard whispers of the Ghost.

People who messed with her tended to disappear.

The underground wasn't safe for anyone. Even healthy people couldn't be trusted. Shielded by rumors, Stella was left alone.

But these patients worried her—people with nothing to lose. She could feel the weight of their stares, oily with sickness. These people who breathed too much of the open air. Most likely, they would die. There was a one in seven chance that dialysis would improve their condition. Some would even make a full recovery.

But some neither recovered nor died. The worst happened to the ones who survived.

Stella walked until she was clear of those stares, through the maze of doors and intersecting tunnels. All the pathways in the city merged into the tunnel where Stella stood now. When the first survivors of the lethal airborne toxins sealed themselves off from the open air, this was where they began to dig. To build. Stella climbed the long spiral staircase of bent iron that led out of the underground city.

At the roof of the staircase, Stella unfastened the dirt-blackened hatch and pulled herself up into the dead world.

She stepped into sand, catching the metal lid before it slammed behind her. Covering her mouth with her hand, Stella sagged against the lid in relief. She exhaled quietly, feeling tension drain out of her.

Why did she feel that the underground was dangerous? She was out in the open—where the monsters lived. What was more, it was getting late. She was running out of time.

The sun was dull orange and low on the dunes, which were barren except for the patches of black weeds. Stella assessed the landscape and found it empty. She was in luck, for now. She bent to pick up the dark hooded jacket she'd stashed by the entrance. It shielded her from the worst of the heat.

Stella set out, following the sound of the low roar and crash of ocean waves. After a quick walk over a high dune, she would arrive at the shoreline. Following the ocean would guide her to her gang's current resting place. She was sweating already. It was significantly cooler down in the tunnels.

It was only when she reached the top of the sandy crest that she noticed the body laid spread-eagle on the shoreline. Stella approached it. She could tell from a distance that its clothes were not yet pillaged. Often, she saw bodies down in the corridors before someone got to carting them away, or even partly submerged here or there in the sand. But a body washed up might be a body that had been tossed into the underground's supply channel—a body that someone wanted to hide. Might still have pills or valuables on it.

Walking closer, Stella realized it had been a man, a tall man. He was built like an ox, with thick muscles coiled under weather-beaten skin. By habit, Stella peered at the man's face, her eyes tracing the stubble on his sturdy jaw. She told herself that she was cautious, that she wasn't looking at his face in particular. One hand inched toward her dagger as she stepped forward and knelt onto the sand. He was handsome. Fascinated by his features, she almost missed the slight flutter under his eyelid.

She hesitated. While there was always the chance that he was infected, there was an equal chance that he was another victim of the city. By his size, she could see him as part of the guards, though he wore a jumpsuit and not a military uniform. He wouldn't be the first guard to end up exiled. Blamed for an outbreak, or for failing to keep their employer alive. The man was covered in sand and alone under the sun's glare. If she left him, he would be helpless. Certainly dead in two and a half hours.

Keeping her dagger at the ready, Stella reached out and tapped the man on his arm. She kept her gaze trained on his eyes, which might burst open, all yellow and frenzied with contamination.

His eyes, when they blinked open, were gray and intelligent. He stared at Stella, his focus sharpening. His cheeks flushed red, which Stella found intriguing. Getting redder, the man tilted his face away.

With one fingernail, Stella guided his chin back to her. Smiling at his shy expression, she asked him, "Why are you here?"

"Sorry. I thought I was dead."

"I thought the same."

He was half-drenched and half-buried. Tanned dark—a color that she would never be able to acquire even if she hadn't coated herself in sunscreen.

"But it appears," the man continued, "that I am alive. I wonder why that is."

"How did you end up here?"

"I'm not entirely sure." He eased himself upright and cupped the back of his head in one large hand. "I think I was attacked. The last thing I remember was..." But the man's voice broke off and he frowned.

Something about him was different. Stella couldn't put her finger on exactly what, just that it was a good difference.

"Sounds like you could use some help," she said. "Would you like to come with me?"

The man dipped his head, averting his eyes, with a trace of a smile set on his lips.

"Yes," he said quietly. "Though, I do need to get back."

"We can sort that out once you're safe," Stella reassured him. He was probably confused. There was no going back to the underground city for him. "Who are you?"

"My name is Gavin. Gavin Owings. And you?"

"I'm Stella Ballare. Can you walk? It's getting late."

Stella grasped his hand, helping him up. His hand was warm, and deeply calloused—though guards did not typically do hard labor. Gavin got to his feet, staggering and clutching at his temple. If he had a head injury, that explained why he seemed a bit disoriented. When he straightened, his full height was striking. She'd seen few others so tall—it revealed a privileged childhood with steady access to nutrition. Not even Xander was this tall.

Gavin trailed Stella across the sand until it gave way to

dusty earth. Save for a handful of abandoned buildings, they could see all the way to the ruins of Manhattan. Some spires and towers of the old city still stood tall. Others had fallen against one another. Left unattended for years, the frameworks had rotted away and collapsed.

Gavin kept looking up, gazing at the sun through the haze of clouds and toxins hanging in the air. They all seemed to do that. Some of the escapees from the underground city were still entranced by the open air for weeks or even months after getting out. Not that Stella blamed them. Fluorescent light was a pale imitation of the brightness and heat of the sun.

He wasn't cowering though. Some city dwellers were used to the tight security of hallways. It was a good thing he wasn't. When people hunched over, afraid of all the open space, it slowed things down. There wasn't time for that. Instead, Gavin gazed at the ruined houses and gutted buildings, unafraid. He seemed curious.

"I've actually never been out in open air before. I had imagined it rather differently." He scanned the horizon. "Where are all the people?"

For as far as the eye could see, there was nothing but desolation, from the rundown cars, swallowed by sand, to the tilted electrical lines.

"Scattered about. Scavenging. Everyone else is underground in the city." As she spoke, Stella noticed how loud their words sounded. Apart from Gavin's voice, she could hear nothing but the light rustle of wind pushing sand over sand. Not the scurry of rats or faint bird calls. Something was wrong.

"Why don't you live in the city?" he asked.

Stella grabbed Gavin's wrist, halting the conversation. She pulled him behind a dusty Nissan Sentra and he crouched awkwardly, mimicking her. Stella peered across the landscape, looking for the source of whatever it was that was making things too quiet.

"Who is that?" Gavin asked her.

Following his line of sight, she spotted it. She tensed, doubling her grip on Gavin's arm. Just twenty feet away, the creature was turned away from them. Half-naked with tell-tale bulging veins. There was still time. If they backed away quietly, it might not notice them.

"Is he all right?" Gavin murmured, propping himself up with one hand against the car frame, straining the rusted metal.

A series of whistles blasted out. Headlights flashed as the Sentra's alarms went off. Gavin jumped back, but it was too late. He just had to lean against a working solar-powered model.

Stella gritted her teeth as the matted blonde head of the creature turned in their direction. Its nostrils flared, breathing in the toxins of the open air—breathing in their scent. Eyes that were solid yellow, from the cornea across the pupils, locked on to her.

Stella knew what Xander would say. *Lose the new guy and hide. He's going to get you killed.*

No. She didn't want to find what was left of him on her next trading trip. She couldn't keep standing aside and watching people die. Not when she could do something about it.

"Run," Stella ordered, pointing Gavin toward the shore.

Gavin raced from the car, but he stopped short when he saw that Stella wasn't following. He hesitated, bracing himself as if he was about to rush back and try to help. Stella stopped him with one fierce glance.

She eased away from the car as the creature leaped on

the hood, crushing out the alarm mechanism with a last flat chirp. Stella took a step back, angling herself away, as the brute growled from deep in the back of its throat.

For one second, there was no movement as the creature smiled wide, revealing its rotting teeth. Then it bellowed, a sound that was all too human and all too close.

Stella tensed, watching with the intensity of a snake charmer. She focused, anticipating its movements, grasping her dagger in a hammer grip.

Then it leaped. With limbs stretched out, Stella could see all the scars running down its body—scars from encounters with its own kind, and from the strain of the airborne contagions. Snakelike, Stella tossed her dagger.

The blade struck neatly into the junction of the neck and shoulder. An incapacitating blow for any normal living thing. Too bad the creature couldn't process pain. Dark blood oozed around the wound, unheeded. The damaged, zombie-like brain registered little besides hunger. The creature landed a few feet away, not slowed down at all.

Should she risk gunfire this close to sundown?

Yellow, frenzied eyes locked on her. The creature crouched low on all fours, tongue lolling out, viscous saliva dripping from its lips.

Screw it.

Stella raised her nine-millimeter Glock, aiming for the head. The shot rang out, echoing far in the quiet. With only a few hours until sundown when the horde awakened.

Any hungry ones would wake now—and the infected always seemed to be hungry.

The creature slumped to the ground. Stella darted forward, pulling her knife free.

Gavin observed the creature with cold, scientific curiosity, just like the stoic nurses with their clipboards scurrying about underground. "What happened to him?"

"The same thing that's about to happen to us. We've got to go." Stella took his hand and ran. The weight of his body jolted her back. Stella held on, dragging him forward until he matched her pace.

Her pill pumped oxygen faster as she demanded more and more from it. Stella's legs burned. She knew from the pressure building in her chest that she had to slow down. Her pill couldn't handle the strain—could even fail on her. Too much pressure and the oxygen pill could burst. The gas released in an explosion that ripped people open from the inside.

If she wasn't fast enough, they would simply be eaten.

She settled for a jog that would have to do. They ran past creatures awakened by the noise. One emerged out of the shadows, stretching and groggy. Stella clenched Gavin's hand, mentally cataloging through places they could hide. Which would mean bunkering down, barricading themselves in through the night.

They jogged a full mile. Far enough away from the gunshot, especially with fresh meat to distract them. It didn't matter to the infected if they ate one of their own. Stella collapsed to her knees, exhaling puffs of carbon dioxide.

Gavin kneeled by her side, placing a tentative hand on her shoulder as her pill stabilized.

"What did you mean?" she asked as soon as she felt normal again. "When you asked what happened to him?" There was no way he didn't know about the airborne toxins. How the infection spread through the bite of those things. Unless he lost his memory somehow?

"Why did he have factory issued pants? Was he newly

turned?" Gavin shook his head, like he couldn't wrap his mind around it.

"Oh. Yeah, that was a new one. Probably ran out of oxygen pills. At that point, once dialysis fails them, they're herded out here with the rest of them."

"That doesn't make sense. We get the census reports and ship out more than enough for everybody."

Stella's mouth fell open.

His jumpsuit had dried in the sun and lost most of the sand covering it in the run. It was a jumpsuit that she'd never seen before, covered in pockets that didn't just swish back and forth as he ran, but also clinked with metals and glass vials. What exactly was she getting herself into?

It clicked. Stella had never seen anyone like him because he didn't belong out here.

She turned to him, swallowing down the shock. "You're from the oxygen factory."

2
_____

Gavin drummed his fingers against the copper pipes as he sighed. Within minutes of arriving at Stella's base, he'd been taken away at gunpoint and locked in a damp holding room with deep scratches crisscrossing the walls.

He had nothing against this quarantine policy. He'd been left unconscious out in the open air. He'd even had close contact with an infected. Transmission of the infection spread through heavy exposure—with a bite. But there was still a slim chance that he still could have gotten contaminated. Respiratory droplets from the creature might have hit his eyes. Gotten inside his mouth.

But they'd held him here for hours.

Symptoms of the infection appeared within an hour, and Gavin showed none of them. His vision was clear, his vitals were stable. Besides, he had no bite marks on him, and he was on a high-capacity oxygen pill.

After the third hour, all this monitoring seemed pointless. He was stuck here with nothing to do.

Across from Gavin, a guard pointed a rifle his way.

Gavin heard the power to the heat pump click on, but the system wasn't running—that would mean the whole facility would only get cold water. He got close enough to the unit to see that the wiring had gotten loose. Not surprising as this room was used to house the infected. It would take him five minutes to set the wires back in order. The click of a rifle stopped him. Gavin opened his mouth to explain himself and stopped at the guard's cold expression. Gavin sat back against the wall and sighed. He hardly noticed the door unlocking, or the soft tread of someone stepping in.

The guard turned his head. Long dreads, tied straight down his back, flapped against his cracked leather jacket. "Don't know why you're bothering with this one. Look at him—he's no fighter, Stella."

At the sound of her name, Gavin looked up and there she was, looking down at him like his own personal guardian angel. His mood brightened, though her arms were crossed. She watched him with a hint of a frown as her eyes lingered on his hunched position.

"Not all of us need to be fighters," she replied.

"Don't mess with him. Xander's already angry," the guard retorted.

"Business as usual, then. Xander's always pissed at me. Here, let me take the next shift." Stella lowered her voice to a murmur, adding, "The antibiotic isn't doing anything. She's asking for you."

A crease formed between the guard's eyebrows. The guard handed off his rifle to Stella, shutting the door behind him. She scooted closer to Gavin, peering into his face. Her eyes were bright violet, framed by snowy lashes.

"Here." Stella pulled a loaf of bread out from under her shirt. "Eat this quick, before someone sees."

Gavin took a bite. He couldn't remember ever feeling so hungry. Or so happy to eat old bread. Stale. But warmed by Stella's body heat... He quickly took another bite before those violet eyes noticed his cheeks flush.

"How are you doing?"

"Better now," Gavin said.

Stella nodded. "I don't think that I can get you home without help. That means getting you into the gang first. Xander's insisting on initiation, and he doesn't like you already."

"Why?"

"Because I brought you in. Or maybe, even if I hadn't, he would have found another reason not to like you."

"What did I ever do to him?" Gavin asked.

"That's just the way he is." Stella shrugged. "Initiations have been getting worse. Our gang is too large. It's tough enough to get food as it is. Xander wants to keep our numbers down."

"What do I have to do to get in?" Gavin asked.

"Kill somebody, kill an infected, bring back food," Stella said.

Gavin buried his face in his palm. Kill somebody? The happy moment he felt at seeing Stella again was long gone. What had he gotten himself into? How was he going to be able to survive?

She rested her hand on his shoulder. The warmth of it in this damp room was... nice. Gavin leaned in closer to her, hoping that she wouldn't take her hand away. She didn't.

"Can you tell me something?" Stella asked.

"About what?" Gavin wished for the right words to say. He wasn't a smooth talker like his brother.

"Tell me about your home. Tell me about where you're from."

"It's kind of big. Noisy." Gavin guessed that this answer wasn't completely the wrong thing to say, as it got a smile out of Stella.

The smile softened her features; all that tense awareness slipped away. It revealed a glimmer of who she could be without the strain of surviving. It wasn't supposed to be this hard.

"Right," Stella said, "but what's so big and noisy about it?"

"Everything in the factory is alive. Even the harvesters are bionic. All those living things have their own noises to them—growing noises, moving sounds, mating calls, chirps, howls. It's the first thing I noticed here. It's so quiet." Gavin leaned his head back, staring at the ceiling tiles. "The factory keeps growing, too. It expands every year."

"I believe that you're from the factory but the others won't."

Gavin ran his fingers through his hair. He had never had to prove who he was to anyone. Everyone knew the quiet son of Arthur Owings back at the factory.

"I doubt anything you could say would convince them. You'll have to find another way," she said.

"Why do I need to convince anyone?"

"It will get them on your side, so someone else out there will try to keep you alive," Stella said. "Do you have pills, by the way?"

Gavin nodded, unzipping a side pocket and pulling out a handful of oxygen pills. Her eyes narrowed when she read the numbers imprinted against the vibrant green. "Last thing I remember, I was clocked in for work in the seaweed fields. I took a double dose." Gavin had actually harvested these pills himself. They were each imprinted with 720—a number for every hour they would work. Unlike other technicians, Gavin preferred the long-term oxygen supply so that he could work without getting distracted by time.

Stella laid her hand over his, brushing his fingers down, closing the pills off from view. "Don't show these to anyone," she warned him, gently holding his hand shut.

The door to Gavin's isolation room opened two hours later, and three men walked in. Gavin's eyes turned to the first man. Not just because Stella and the others automatically looked to him, but because Gavin recognized power in his presence—it was the same way that people reacted to his own father.

From the man's square jaw, marred by scars, to the blonde hair and pale eyes, to his broad solid shoulders, there was an unspoken authority that hung about him. Gavin didn't need to see the gun holstered at his side, underneath his militaristic jacket, to know he was dangerous.

So this must be Xander.

Xander strode into the room, stopping when he saw Stella still sitting unarmed next to Gavin. "What are you doing here?" he said to her.

"Guarding him," Stella said.

Xander scowled. "Get out."

She strode up to Xander and placed a hand lightly on his forearm. Gavin couldn't help but notice the hint of a smile on the man's face at Stella's touch.

"I brought this one in for a reason," she said. "He's my responsibility."

Xander paused, looking carefully at the contours of Stella's face, before he pointed to the back of the room where the other two men stood. Stella joined them without another word.

"How did you get so big?" Xander asked, sizing Gavin up.

"From working. I specialize in mechanical engineering," Gavin replied.

"Yes, but what did you eat? How did you get the meat?" Xander circled near with all the confidence and aggression of an alpha wolf.

"I'm a vegetarian," Gavin said. Before he could react, Xander's fist latched on to the front of his uniform to slam him back against the wall. Pain convulsed through him as the tender bruise at the back of his head crashed against concrete.

"Answer the damn question," Xander snapped. More than the pain, Gavin felt a numb surprise.

"Vegetarian means I don't eat meat. Just food made from plants." Gavin watched the man without seeming to, wary and focused on his movements without looking directly at him. It was a trick that worked when he needed to tranquilize the bulls.

"Don't mess with me," Xander warned.

Gavin shrugged in reply. As Xander released his grip, Gavin saw a wariness in Xander that mirrored his own. Something about the way he was reacting was not what Xander expected from him. Gavin thought back to his conversation with Stella, trying to pinpoint what sort of answer Xander wanted to hear.

"My father's in charge where I work, so it isn't as if I've ever been without food," Gavin said.

"Then how did you end up here?" came Xander's next question, the same question Gavin had been asking himself, trying to think back. He couldn't remember anything out of the ordinary before waking up out on the sand.

"I don't know."

Xander's clenched fist struck toward him again, and this

time Gavin reacted, catching it easily in his own calloused hand.

Behind Xander, the other two men aimed pistols at him. Stella tensed, with her hands clenched into fists.

"If you don't want me here, I'll go," Gavin said.

Xander strained against him, testing his strength. He stopped all at once, smirking. "So you do have some fight in you. Maybe we can find a way to use you after all."

Gavin let go of his hold and crossed his arms over his chest uneasily, not trusting Xander's sudden change.

"If you want in the gang, and the security that goes with it, I'll run you through a test first." There was something off about Xander's casual tone. "Go into New York and bring back a food shipment."

"That's at least a two-man job," Stella called out.

"Are you volunteering?" The challenge in Xander's tone was unmistakable, as he turned his back on Gavin to stare her down.

Stella paused for so long that Gavin thought that she wasn't going to answer. In a soft voice she said, "Yes."

Xander approached Stella, glaring down at her petite frame. "Why?"

"I want him alive," she said.

"If you want him alive so bad, you just go on right ahead." Xander stepped around her and strode out of the room. The other men lowered their weapons and followed.

As soon as Stella spoke up, it was clear that Xander's problem wasn't really about Gavin at all. Xander and Stella's interactions didn't follow the behaviors of the others in the gang. Stella wasn't expected to blindly follow his orders. As if she was outside of the power dynamic of the group. Not in charge. But free to do what she wanted, in a way the others were not.

Gavin felt pressure at the crook of his elbow and looked down to see a slender hand tugging his arm. He looked up to see Stella's brilliant violet eyes fixed on him.

"Come on, Gavin. Let's get you ready."

Gavin allowed himself to be led, the small hands continuing to rest on his arm.

"WE DON'T HAVE MUCH TIME TO PRACTICE." SHE WAS LOADING bullets into the magazine one by one, methodically. The humor that Gavin had seen traces of since they had met was gone. She had lined up a can on top of the concrete ledge that made up part of the hotel barricades.

"Did I get you in trouble?" Gavin asked.

"Everyone knows that New York is a suicide mission— it's completely infested," Stella explained. "Xander was just letting me know that if I choose to help you, he's not going to stop me. He's telling me that I'm making the choice to die."

"I'm not asking you to..." Gavin began, but Stella cut him off.

"And I'm not planning on dying. I'll think of something." She slipped the magazine into her handgun, cocking it. She held the nine-millimeter Glock centered in the web of her hand, between her thumb and fingers, with the ease of long familiarity. "I've known Xander for seven years, and he's never been this angry with me," she admitted, lowering the gun. She shook her head.

Exactly how close was Stella with Xander?

She handed the weapon back to Gavin, gesturing at the targets. Gavin mimicked her hold on the gun, bracing himself for the overwhelming power of it. Tension rippled through him, and Gavin had to force himself back into calm. It was a tool and nothing more. Target and fire. His fingers clenched down on the trigger, and Gavin ignored the jolt of it, firing. His bullets hit their mark. Gavin shattered the can that Stella had set up for target practice. Despite all his protests that he was nonviolent, Gavin had taken to the gun like he was a machine.

"Good. Let's see how you do at loading it on empty. You press the magazine release." Stella demonstrated, dropping the spent magazine to the ground. "Don't point the gun away; keep it on the target. Slide in the new one." Stella pulled a fresh magazine out of her pocket and locked it in place. "Cock it, and fire before you get eaten alive." She handed the loaded gun back to him.

Gun in hand, he paused, sorting through the steps in his mind until he got it right. He aimed at a stop sign in the distance, concentrating on the space in the middle of the *O*. Then he focused, blocking out everything. Nothing was left except the target, the task, and the familiar feel of metal. Gavin fired to his last bullet, smoothly loading a new magazine just as Stella had shown him.

He didn't stop until he fired the last bullet in the clip. With the job done, Gavin became aware of the dull throb in his hand, the ringing in his ear, and the fact that he had acquired an audience.

"Looks like you haven't lost it after all." Gavin turned to see the man with the dreads once again, speaking to Stella. "You still know how to pick them, Stella."

"Found you, didn't I?" Stella replied with an amused half-grin. When he didn't answer, the smile dropped from her face. Her voice lowered to a conspiratorial whisper. "How is she doing, Sam?"

"Same." Sam stared at the hole that Gavin had blasted away into the stop sign.

"I'll stop in after training," Stella said.

Sam nodded and headed back into the gang's base—a boarded-down, fortified hotel that remained somewhat untouched by the typical damage brought on by the scavenging infected.

"We're done?" Gavin asked. He had only shot three clips. Surely he needed more practice before going out to face what was out there.

"If we practice for much longer, it'll wake the infected. Shooting is always a risk, even this early in the day. The sound travels for miles. Besides, there's more I need to show you."

Stella led him back inside, through a staircase down to the basement. They walked past the boiler room where he'd been quarantined, with the flat clicking of the malfunctioning heat pump. Down the hallway, to a grimy room half filled with rotted furniture.

"Do you trust me?" she asked.

He probably would have gotten eaten without her. "Yes."

Stella smiled, her pale lips parting over even, white teeth. "Then put this over your eyes." She held out a white folded cloth.

Gavin placed the material over his eyes, feeling it tighten as Stella tied it in a knot at the back of his head, blinding him.

"This is the way my father taught me," Stella said from somewhere in front of him. "The infected are blind. Learn to move like them. Learn to think like them. It'll keep you alive." Her voice seemed to come from somewhere else now. When she wasn't speaking, her presence slipped away from Gavin into nothingness.

"Come find me," she said.

All he was aware of was his own heavy footfall as he took a step in the direction he last heard her voice. At least he thought she was in that direction. The world around him was empty, except for the hum of electricity.

Was he always so loud? Each step was a thud. The rustle of his clothes. The jangle of supplies in his pockets. Each sound was a new piece of information. Gavin had been born in a world full of noise. Normally, he focused on tuning it out.

He treaded lighter, painfully aware of every motion: the light scuff of his boot against the concrete floor, the crunch of dirt under his foot. That noise was surely loud enough to bring the infected running from wherever they were hiding.

Gavin stopped at the point where he had heard Stella's voice last. He hesitated, unable to hear anything in front of him. As they had both taken oxygen pills, he couldn't even hear the sounds of their breathing.

"I'm here," Stella said softly.

Gavin felt the light touch of her fingertips trail against his outstretched arms. He started, wanting to rip the cloth away from his eyes. Gavin's heart beat faster, though the touch was quick and light.

Hesitantly, Gavin reached for her, grasping her small hand. Her fingers interlocked with his. Without his sight to get in the way, he focused on the warmth of her hand, the smooth texture of it.

"How are you so quiet?" Gavin asked.

"Practice."

Gavin was sure she was smiling again, even though he didn't see her face. Then those little fingers slipped away, as if Stella had disappeared.

"Find me again." Stella's voice came from a different corner of the room.

Gavin locked in on the sound of her voice, picturing her location. Stepping carefully to dull the sound of his footsteps, Gavin sought her out.

It was easy to forget that he was training for a suicide mission when all he wanted to do was seek out the touch of her soft skin.

3

"Thanks again for guarding him." Stella said, after glancing down the bend of the stairway to make sure they were alone. The back stairway was rarely used, but it didn't hurt to be careful. She'd left Gavin in an abandoned midlevel room, with the suggestion that he practice moving stealthily. There was no need to antagonize Xander further by parading Gavin around in the dining hall.

Sam shook his head. "Almost wish I hadn't. You're risking too much for this guy."

"You heard about New York?"

"Everyone's heard about New York. Paul bet Dan his stash of green beans that Xander's bluffing."

It was the one place Stella swore she'd never return to. Xander really had it out for Gavin, giving him New York for his initiation. No one with half a functioning human brain went into the city.

Stella shook her head. "Xander doesn't back down from the rules. Not for anybody."

"He's more likely going to try to off him in the night. Or push a new partner on him first thing in the morning.

Someone like Ben, who'll take him a few miles out to feed the infected."

"That's why I'm leaving at first light."

Sam's eyes widened. "That's against the rules."

"I know the rules, I taught him the rules. It's not my fault Xander took them all to extremes."

"You really are going to get yourself killed." Sam cursed in a low tone. "Stella, why are you doing this?"

Stella peered around the stairway listening intently. She dropped her voice. "If you weren't guarding him, he'd be dead already."

"Why? What's he got on him?" Sam said, in a low voice.

Typically new recruits were body searched. Anything suspicious would be taken from them and reported to Xander. But if the supplies were really good? It would be easy enough to steal pills and valuables. All they'd have to do was shoot the newcomer and claim that they were showing signs of turning.

"He's got oxygen pills numbered with three digits. I think he's carrying over a year's supply. Not the standard pills either, the high-grade stuff."

"Are you serious? Who is this guy, some kind of thief? He got connections or something?"

"He got it straight from the source."

"Straight from the... are you talking about the *factory*? Stella, that's not possible."

"Get him talking about any kind of science and see for yourself. He's not from here."

"This sounds crazy." Sam shook his head. "You sure you're not just distracted by his pretty face."

"His what?" Stella rolled her eyes. "No. That's not what this is about."

"You're so defensive. No wonder Xander's jealous."

"He's got nothing to be jealous about. The only man I ever loved was my father," Stella said, brushing aside Sam's comments.

"Sure doesn't look that way, seeing how you're always holding his hand." Sam smirked when she glared at him.

They walked down the length of the stairway, listening by the door that led to the dining hall. It was quiet. They were early enough to avoid the rush. Stela could grab enough food for the trip and slip away unseen.

"You really think he's from the factory, then?" Sam raised an eyebrow.

"I do, and it complicates things." Stella sighed.

"How so?"

"What would you do with someone from the oxygen factory?" Stella murmured.

"I don't know." Sam frowned, mulling it over. "Try to get them to give me pills. Maybe even get them to build something. Someone like that has got to improve survival chances."

"Exactly. Anyone who gets their hands on him will try to use him." The only problem was that keeping him alive without revealing what he could do was turning into a challenge.

"What do you plan to do with him?"

The first time she had seen Gavin, he had looked into her face and blushed. He was so quick to admit that he trusted her. His naiveté would get him killed in the wrong hands.

"I want to keep him alive. Help him get home."

"Can't you take him back now instead of risking his life in New York?"

If only it were that simple. "The only way I can think of to get him back to the oxygen factory is straight through the heart of the underground. How am I supposed to get him through the underground city without help?" But it was more than that. People didn't just end up washed up on a shore randomly. Something bad happened to him, and Stella doubted it was safe to send him back without figuring out how he ended up here in the first place.

Opening the double doors, Stella saw the one man she had attempted to avoid all night. As soon as she stepped through, his eyes locked on her. She didn't even have a chance to turn back before Xander got up, crossing through the rows of tables over to her.

Sam murmured, "I'll take him with me." Then he walked over to the food, crossing to the other side of the room to avoid Xander.

The muscles in her legs tensed as Xander approached, stopping in front of her. He nodded toward the exit, gesturing for her to follow.

THEIR ARGUMENT OVER GAVIN WAS FRESH IN HER MIND.

She followed Xander to the rooftop, neither of them saying a word on the way. Xander walked straight to the edge and held the rail, staring into the horizon. Stella joined his side, looking out across the desert sands to see what he saw.

Here, from twelve stories up, the buildings still standing in New York City were clearly visible.

So that's how it was. He was playing on her fears.

"How long has it been since the last time you've been out there?" he asked her. "Five years?"

Stella didn't reply. He knew how long it had been.

"It's gotten worse. I haven't gone in a year myself. Don't

even know how bad it is now."

At least he still cared if she lived or not.

Out here in the sunlight, away from the others, it was easier to remember who Xander used to be. He caught her looking over at him. "What are you thinking?"

"I wish we could go back to how things were. You were my best friend." When she'd first seen Xander, he was just a kid, struggling for fifteen minutes to open a can of Campbell's chicken and dumplings with a dull knife.

He brushed his fingers against her cheek, lacing them into her hair. "I don't want to be friends."

"That's not very nice." Stella pulled away, choosing to misinterpret him. She looked down, as if hurt by his words.

"People change, Stella."

"I know. I just didn't want us to change." There was a time when she would have wanted to be with him. Before he'd evolved into this unyielding man who wouldn't change his own rules even to save someone he cared about.

"Please don't go," Xander murmured, revealing a trace of who he used to be.

She scooted closer to him and rested her head against his arm like she used to do when they were kids. "I can't sit back and watch this one die," Stella whispered. When she felt his arm tense, she reassured him. "You know me. I'll be fine."

Xander hesitated, then pulled her into a hug.

When he let her go, he nodded as though he had decided something.

He unlocked the roof's equipment shed, what he called his back-up plan, showing Stella a weapons cache filled with automatic rifles, ammo, and even hand grenades.

"Take what you need," Xander said, "and make sure that you come back."

4
———

After their practice, Gavin was aware of every sound—the footsteps, electrical clicks, and even gunshots in the distance.

Gavin practiced walking quietly, until his steps were less lumbering. They were about as noiseless as he could hope for, before he stopped and stood awkwardly. What would he say if someone asked him what he was doing? He leaned against the wall with his arms crossed, waiting.

As the back of his head touched the wall, he recalled a flash of blue—undersea, where he was last in the oxygen factory. He was in the seaweed fields surrounded by spiraling strands of kelp. He was taking samples from kelp that glowed with a genetically altered luminescence. Something was reflected in the metal of his syringe, something that surprised him. He couldn't make out the reflection before the memory slipped away.

The doors to the room opened and Stella's friend Sam came in.

"Come on. I've got to get back." Sam held a tray of pasta

without sauce and pickles that were discolored in the center. Gavin didn't miss the look of suspicion on Sam's face.

Sam, like Stella, walked through the hotel hallways with caution. He paused at doorways, listening, before silently motioning Gavin on. Was this creeping around some sort of entrenched survival mechanism from living for years among the infected? Or was this his fault? Hopefully Sam was showing extra caution because Xander disliked newcomers who hung around Stella. If this was how Sam always walked around his gang, it meant he didn't think he could trust the others.

"Stella said you're some kind of scientist?" Sam said in a low voice, when he was sure they were alone.

"Not really."

"What does that mean?" Sam narrowed his eyes. "Either you are, or you aren't."

"I can't really say I'm a scientist because I'm not conducting any of the research. Not for the clinical trials, or the search for the cure."

"What do you do?"

Gavin dug into his pocket for one of his pills. He tapped out a sequence on its outer shell. The pill expanded to full size, roughly the height of an oxygen tank.

"I spend a lot of time harvesting, and with quality control. It's a delicate bit of machinery. The pill needs to be able to do a lot of things. It compresses, to fit down the trachea, you know," Gavin slid his finger down the front of his throat. "The windpipe. It also has to numb all the muscles involved naturally with breathing." Gavin pointed to clockwork mechanisms and intricate gears. "This part releases oxygen and sets out alarms when it's close to empty."

Gavin turned the pill in his hand, frowning. "I'm trying

to fine tune the design, but the pill was never meant to be a permanent solution. Most of the research back home is focused on the cure."

"Put that away. Shrink it, quick." Sam hissed.

Gavin blinked in surprise. He repeated the sequence on the pill's outer shell and pocketed it once the pill had shrunk back down.

"I thought Stella had lost it, for sure." Sam muttered. "You really are from the factory." Sam crossed the hallway to one of the hotel rooms and pulled out a key. He unlocked it and entered the room, leaving the door ajar. "Come in. Lock the door behind you."

Inside, the layout of the room was nearly identical to the one Stella had left him practicing in. Limp curtains against the window. Bed. The electric hum of a mini refrigerator. A round table in the back was laden with medical supplies. There were pill bottles, discolored and covered in grime. Had Sam found those supplies out in the ruined city? They had to be expired. Some medications would still be effective, though less potent. But why wouldn't they just use the regular supplies they sent to the underground city?

"Can you help her?" Sam said from the back of the room, partially out of view.

A girl lay limp on the couch. Her black curls were damp and plastered against round cheeks. Cold sweat broke out against the dainty features of a lovely face, made haunting by the pallor and sunken eyes. A red trickle slipped out from under her nose, which Sam wiped carefully away.

Could this be a reaction to the airborne toxins? Gavin ran through the typical symptoms he had encountered in toxin simulations: fever, sure, but also skin and eye discolorations, which she didn't have. He'd heard of her symptoms before. They were complications from something.

Why couldn't he remember? What happened to his memory during his accident?"

Something clicked into place—Gavin remembered where he had seen this condition before.

"I have something that could help," Gavin unzipped his breast pocket, taking out a vial filled with a sky-blue liquid.

Sam eyed the blue liquid blankly. "You're sure?"

Gavin nodded, rubbing the back of his neck. He had used this hundreds of times with the same results. Though he'd never had an audience before.

Sam kissed the girl's knuckles and then stood, walking out of the way. Making room.

From closer up, it was clear that the girl was suffering from an increased reaction to the toxins. This would work.

Measuring a few drops into a syringe carefully, Gavin felt the weight of Sam's gaze. As Gavin disinfected the injection area at the girl's arm, Sam clenched his fist, but didn't say a word or make any move to stop him. Gavin administered the injection, plunging medicine into her system.

In the time it took him to withdraw the needle and put away his supplies, the drug took hold, with a subtle shift from sickness to health. The girl's face regained color, enough for Gavin to see that there was an olive tone to her skin. Her lips, too, seemed to grow pinker. Fuller. She began to stir.

Sam knelt in front of her. "Natalia? Nat?"

Her eyes flicked open in reply, and Gavin was startled to see that they were a honey color. Similar to the solid yellow eyes of the infected, though hers were light and clear. Natural.

"Hey," Sam said gently. "You okay?"

Natalia smiled at him in answer.

"Let me know if she needs another dose later. Should be

fine now, though," Gavin mumbled, hoping not to draw attention back to himself. His words were lost on the pair by the couch as Sam pulled Natalia carefully into a hug.

Gavin blushed at the whispered endearments from the couch. He scanned the room for something to do.

The light fixture was flickering. Gavin grabbed a chair and stood on it, fiddling with the loose connections causing the issue.

There. Fixed.

"Thank you," Natalia called out to Gavin, in a somewhat weak voice. "For whatever it was you gave me."

"Oh," Gavin said. "You're welcome."

"Are you some sort of doctor?"

Gavin shook his head. "No, I just work with doctors."

"Do you know what's wrong with me? What did you give me?"

"You're showing symptoms of immune suppression. An increased vulnerability to viruses, bacteria, and the toxins. That compound I gave you boosts the immune system."

"Immune... suppression? How did that happen?"

"There's a couple common conditions and diseases that can compromise the immune system," Gavin said. "How long were you sick?"

"A few weeks. Past couple of days, I just kept getting worse." Natalia leaned against the faded velvet of the couch. "Sam was worried that we wouldn't be able to hide it much longer."

"You don't have any stiffness in your joints or wrists?"

Natalia frowned and shook her head.

"No increased thirst? Or blurred vision?"

"No," Natalia said in a small voice.

"What did it start with?"

"Before it got worse," Natalia said, "I felt nauseous all the time. Threw up a bit."

"Oh. Well, women's immune systems can get weakened if their bodies are suppressing a response to paternal genetic material... during pregnancy."

Sam and Natalia turned to each other, wide-eyed.

"When was the last time?" Sam stroked her arm, reassuringly. But his voice was tense.

"It's been a while, but I don't always get it," Natalia's voice got lower, "Stress makes it go sometimes."

"So it could be?"

Natalia held her forehead in her hand and was looking out into nothing, just thinking.

"I'm dead," she said in a flat voice.

Tension knotted its way through Gavin, sinking heavily into the pit of his stomach. Dead? What was she talking about? "No. You aren't going to die. That boost should keep most of the effects of the toxins away."

Sam swept a curl behind Natalia's ear with shaky hands.

"Broke the rules." Natalia shook her head numbly. "Going to get kicked out. I'm already an exile from the underground. There's nowhere left to go."

5

When Stella got to Nat's room, she felt the tension as soon as Sam opened the door for her. Sam let her in automatically before giving her a double take.

"Where did you get that?" He pointed to the rifles slung across her back.

"Xander."

"Only you could get into a fight with him and still get special treatment," Sam mumbled.

He didn't even know about the hand-grenades and ammo in her pockets.

Sam dragged his hands across his hair and avoided eye contact.

What's going on?

"Nat!" Stella's mouth fell open, as tears welled in the corners of her eyes. Natalia was sitting upright. Her skin had regained color from the ashen sickly state she had before.

Stella had been so worried that Natalia wasn't going to make it. She'd lost so many friends. Couldn't take losing Natalia, too.

Though sitting upright, Natalia was hunched on the sofa with her knees drawn up to her chest. She looked dazed.

Stella crossed the room and grasped Natalia's hand in both of hers. "What's wrong?"

For a tense moment, no one replied. Then Natalia whispered, "I think I'm pregnant," before bursting into tears.

Stella rubbed reassuring circles on her back. "It's all right. We can fix this." Stella dropped her voice low. "I know someone in the city who could take care of it."

With a little make-up to hide Natalia's tattoo and enough oxygen pills, Stella would be able to get Natalia into one of the medical facilities in the underground city. It was a simple enough procedure. Her contact shouldn't give her too much trouble over it.

"I don't want to get rid of it," Natalia said.

It was as if the temperature in the room dropped ten degrees. What did that mean? Was Natalia considering having the baby? Xander would never allow her to stay.

Stella didn't miss the quick, irritated look that Sam shot at Gavin, and she winced.

"So what do you want to do?" Stella had to make sure that she wasn't misinterpreting Natalia.

"I want to try to let my baby live."

"Even if it means getting kicked out?" Relocation was just the first issue Natalia would have to face.

Babies were loud. She'd have to find someplace relatively soundproof and secure enough to withstand the horde. If there was such a place.

"Yes. If I have to leave, I'll go." Natalia stared at the space in front of her.

"All right." Stella squeezed Natalia's hands. "Nobody knows yet. You can hide it. There's still time."

Her heart pounded as her throat went dry. Sam and

Natalia. Her two closest friends. She was losing both of them. "I have a supply of oxygen pills hidden in my locker. Take it. Maybe use it to trade your way into another gang."

None of the others had rules as strict as Xander. But then again, none of the others were as effective at keeping people alive.

Natalia blinked rapidly, holding back tears. She nodded.

"We'll get going, then. I'll think of something." Stella rubbed the back of her neck, trying to ease the building tension.

Natalia grabbed her hand before Stella could move away. "You need to take care of yourself in the city. Be careful."

Stella nodded, not trusting herself to say another word.

STELLA DIDN'T SPEAK TO GAVIN UNTIL THEY HAD REACHED HER room on the eighth floor. As soon as the door had shut them in, she questioned him. "What did you say to her?"

"Just that I'd help her if I could."

"Why would you say that?" Stella stepped in front of her desk, staring at the photograph that was the only thing that marked this room as her own.

"Because it's a baby." The way Gavin's voice strained over the last word reminded her that she was dealing with someone who was different. He didn't know any better.

"I'm not saying that killing babies is the right thing to do. I'm just saying that instead of letting one person die, you've talked her into letting three people die." Stella shook her head, as if the motion would be able to dislodge the image of Sam and Natalia with a screaming newborn. A pack of the infected tearing into them like so many vultures.

"Then they shouldn't be kicked out. Babies don't have to mean the death of their parents," Gavin argued.

"I did the same thing to my mother. I was loud. I cried. And she died for it," Stella said with her back to him, wondering why she was even telling him this.

Stella never talked about her mother.

She stared at the photograph of her mother and father holding her. She'd never know the woman she resembled so much.

"I meant what I said," Gavin told her. "I want to help."

The raw honesty in his voice drained the rest of her anger away.

"Just try to get some sleep, Gavin," she murmured. "We leave at first light." She placed a blanket on the couch. It was too small for him, but she couldn't leave him with Sam anymore like she had originally planned. Her room would have to do.

Like many nights before a scavenging trip, Stella couldn't sleep. Stella peered out her window, just able to make out the silhouette of a pack of infected as they roamed the night, hunting for their nocturnal prey. Stella looked back to where Gavin tossed and turned on her couch and sighed.

When did it get so hard to have friends? She'd stopped making new friends long ago. It was too hard when she lost them.

Boar brush in hand, Stella inspected the equipment and scrubbed out the barrel. When the equipment was in order, she traced imaginary lines into the table in the best approximations of the layout of the city. She planned out the safest routes.

Gavin's initiation had turned into a battle of wills

between her and Xander. This wasn't the first time he'd raised the stakes, pressuring Stella to give in.

Xander probably expected her to back down in the morning. Or maybe Sam was right, and he'd try to force Gavin to partner up with one of his goons, who would just take him far enough away and shoot him in the back.

But Xander wouldn't act until the sun was fully up. Stella and Gavin would be far away by then.

She couldn't stand by and do nothing. What was the point of soldiering on if she had to lose everyone she cared about to do it? She couldn't keep losing people.

In the morning, she placed a hand on Gavin's shoulder. "Hey, wake up." The first red sun rays pierced through the blinds of her window, bathing his face in strips of light. She waited to see his eyes open, clear gray and confused as they looked around before they settled on her.

"Morning," Stella greeted him, holding back a smile as he held her gaze.

She stepped to the supplies laid out on her desk, listening to Gavin getting out of bed and following her. Wordlessly, she handed him a pistol and a drawstring bag. It was filled with all the survival necessities: sunscreen, basic first aid, freeze-dried rations, a canteen, a switchblade, and the ever-useful duct tape. Stella hoisted her own bag across her shoulder, pausing a moment to look at her parents' picture before slipping that in with the rest of her supplies. She never left her parents behind for long.

The hotel was quiet as the two of them walked down the corridors and stairwell. Before she knew it, she was at the entrance, her hand poised over the lock, about to step into danger once again. She felt a pounding in her heart that echoed in the ticking pressure within her lungs as her oxygen pill matched the demands of her body. She closed her eyes for a moment, relishing this one last measure of calm before stepping outside.

Her leather shoes sank noiselessly into the sand. Behind her, she heard the light crunch of Gavin's boots. The sun hung low, just breaking the world out of the shadows, and the night-hunting infected would be turning to their shelter. Assuming they had caught something in the dark.

A rat scuttled by the hotel foundation. It disappeared in a flash of pale fur and a dirt-streaked tail, slipping away between the cracks. Rats would stay hidden if they could smell an infected near.

The tension in her shoulders eased.

"You ready?" Stella asked Gavin, with a half-smile that she was sure didn't reach her eyes. "Just stay close."

Seeing Gavin nod, Stella led them to the remaining patches of asphalt that made up the road into the city.

Sam's words echoed in Stella's head. *Can't you take him back now instead of risking his life in New York?* Now that they were actually on their way, Sam's words began to sound better and better.

"Where is the oxygen factory?" Stella asked Gavin.

"Deep under the ocean," Gavin replied. "Where the infected can't get to it."

"How far?"

"Fifteen minutes by submarine to the city, at forty knots. Multiply by one-point-fifteen, divide by four..." Gavin's index finger pointed at the numbers he could see in his mind. "So that's eleven-point-five miles away."

"Could you swim that?" Stella sized up the broad muscles across his shoulders and back, thinking that he, if anyone, had a shot of swimming down into the black waters with just the right oxygen pill and some diving gear.

"If I didn't get eaten along the way."

Stella didn't have to ask what would try to eat him. She had seen enough of the way the toxins had impacted the surviving wildlife, seen enough of the overgrown and lethal combinations of mutations on land. If the same was happening under the ocean waves, it was something she didn't want to ever encounter.

"New York it is, then," Stella muttered resignedly.

"You never told me why you don't live underground with the other survivors," Gavin said, reminding her that, yes, if she really didn't want to take Gavin into New York, there was still one more option.

The thought of Gavin in the tunnels... They'd stand more of a chance against the infected in New York than the administrators in the city. At least she could understand the motivations of the infected; hunger she understood very well.

She couldn't blame anything as simple as survival as the reason the administrators did what they did.

"I've never lived underground, and I wouldn't live there if I had any other choice," Stella said, muting her feelings.

"But wouldn't you be safer underground? We send supplies; you wouldn't have to go searching for food like this."

"The people underground are powerless. Here, at least I have a gun." Seeing Gavin's confused look, she explained further. "Everything is monitored by the administrators. Yes, the administrators provide everything. Food. Pills. Clothes. But one mistake and they take everything away."

"That's not the way it is supposed to work," Gavin said.

"Natalia was our most recent one. When she worked as a nurse underground, too many of her patients survived, even the ones who weren't supposed to. The administration started cutting down her food rations. She could either help poison the administration's targets or starve to death. So she chose the desert."

"Couldn't that just have been a mistake?" Gavin asked. To Stella, he sounded just like a citizen who believed in systems, believed that life was fair—until it happened to them.

"Sam was an electrical technician. After a power failure at the administrators' lounge, the electricians on duty had their pills cut for a week. We were there for supplies, and he just joined the raid. Escaped with us. Those are just the two people you know. Everyone in the gang has a story." Stella knew every last one of those stories. If Gavin had to be convinced, she could let him know all about the corruption underground, from what went on in the entertainment district to the people denied oxygen pills until they began to sicken.

"What about you? You said you never lived under-ground. Did the city screw up your life, too?"

"Yes. It did." Stella hadn't meant for her words to sound so bleak. This time she couldn't hide the trace of her rage.

Gavin didn't ask any more questions.

They followed the road, where they could see the cracked pieces of asphalt sticking out from beneath sand. They passed the ruins of cars, some still filled with sun-melted bodies that had been left to cook behind the glass since the time of infection. According to a road sign, with its high-carbon-steel pole bent at a low angle, they were trav-eling on I-95.

Here, along the side of the road, vegetation grew in dark patches. These plants had an adverse reaction to the toxins, and the animals—or people—that ate them regularly would build up a lethal concentration of poisons in their systems.

Gavin looked at everything as if he were cataloging

details for later use. "What makes New York so dangerous?" he finally asked.

"The freezers."

Gavin did a double take, raising his eyebrows.

Stella explained, "There are still working freezers in the city. It's one of the few places for miles that still has viable food, even if the infected aren't too skilled at getting at it. Still attracts them from all around."

"So how are we going to survive?" Gavin asked softly.

Stella slowed her brisk pace, considering. For all the raw power in his muscular physique, there was vulnerability in his words. Others who came out here, out in the open, out in the heat, seemed stripped down to a primal essence. Nothing left in them but the cruel instinct to live. His quiet concern was incomparable.

Waiting for her reply, Gavin's posture was stiff. He rubbed the back of his neck as he scanned their surroundings for unfamiliar danger. Stella closed the distance between the two of them, tracing a hand up to his shoulder, comforting him.

Her stomach was tense, and she couldn't shake the image of the hordes of New York. But she was done with standing back and doing nothing.

"To make it, you've got to know their habits."

"Tell me, please," Gavin said with a hint of a smile.

"Don't underestimate their blindness. If they can hear you, they know exactly where you are. If you stand still, they can sniff you out. That's the first mistake people make."

"What do you do if one finds you?"

"Outsmart it. If that doesn't work, shoot its brains out and hide," Stella said with a grim relish, pulling out her handgun and miming the kill: aim, fire, and the jerk of feedback at the end of it.

Their path was clear all the way to the bridge. The sand yielded to smooth concrete. They rounded a corner, passing a sign that announced that the GWB Southwalk was open between the hours of 6 a.m. to midnight, and then there it was.

Criss-crossed steel towers dominated the view. Silence fell over them as they neared the colossal architecture—the barrel cables and their protection shields. The remnants of a time before oxygen pills.

They walked over level concrete, the spray of the Hudson River misting over them. Except for the low rail separating them from the water below, the walkway looked like a typical sidewalk. Once Stella began to move, she felt the unsettling sensation of being suspended in space without solid ground beneath her. The railing did little to shield her view of the air beneath them, or, a fair distance below that, of the water sandwiched between rocky cliffs.

Stella closed her eyes against the vertigo, focusing on their path.

"There's the city," Stella said in a low voice. Gavin held on to the rail, looking out across the expanse of the George Washington to the rise of the buildings in the distance. All they could see were the skyscrapers, calm and still. From the bridge, they wouldn't be able to see all of those openings— all the cracked windows, the doors, the alleyways. There were thousands of places for the infected to hide in every direction. Stella shifted the mesh bag on her shoulder, hearing the reassuring clink of ammunition and grenades.

Gavin tensed beside her, staring into the mirror that reflected what was coming along around the bend. He reached for the gun holster, his fingers hovering over the metal.

Stella brushed her hand over his, feeling the rough

texture and stopping him. She removed her hand, lifting one finger to her lips for silence. She had seen it, too.

Silently, she slipped ahead in quick, light steps. She rested her hand on a weather-beaten sign hanging on by corroded screws, testing its hold.

An infected stepped around the corner into view. The tattered remains of its shirt did little to cover a female body, burnt by the sun's glare and ripped apart internally by the spread of toxins. Long curly hairs remained on the head in patches, screening half of the blind face of the infected from view. Stella could see, even under the strands of hair, the movement of nostrils as they flared wide and the thing took in their scent. She waited for its tell, the moment between walking and hunting. She saw it in the twitch of stiff hands a second before the creature charged their way.

Stella grasped the National Suicide Prevention Lifeline sign with the message "You're not alone," ripped it clear off the rail, and slammed it into the skull of the infected. Its head whipped back. Carried by the momentum, its body toppled over the rail. Stella leaned over the metal bars to view the descent, watching the threat become smaller and smaller until it slammed into the black water below.

Gavin joined her side, staring at the ripples in the water, all that was left of the encounter. He smiled at her tentatively, but his eyes were tight with tension. She understood his worry. Even here, far from the city and early in the day, they were already running into the infected.

Stella grasped the sign tight, holding it away from her as blood slipped off the dented aluminum. She might need it again.

Each new step brought the buildings closer. They passed the second tower of the bridge, almost to the point where the crosswalk curved around to the exit ramp. She stopped, pulling two filthy shirts, torn and stained by things she didn't want to think about. The grime of it left behind an oily residue on her hands and a nasty, crawling feeling.

"Here, put this on." She handed Gavin one shirt and put hers on, trying not to think about what she was doing. When Gavin took the fabric in his hand and grimaced, Stella explained, "It'll hide our scent."

After Gavin pulled the shirt on, Stella looked him in the eye. "Anything could happen in there. If we're separated," she said, not mentioning the specific scenarios already churning through her thoughts, "get out. Get back here. I'll try to meet you here. If I don't, run. Put as much distance between you and the city as you can."

A crease formed in between his eyebrows as he considered the possibility of leaving her behind. Stella doubted that he would, no matter what she told him.

As the Southwalk curved, descending into New York's 178th Street, Stella thought over their route one last time, going over her mental map of the city. Adrenaline thudded through her system, wiring her for action. Yet she forced herself to step with care down the remainder of the walkway and forced herself to look for signs of the infected. The building to her right had fresh blood on the walls. Windows were trashed, broken into with fragments of glass hanging onto wooden frames. On the street corner was a pile of droppings that looked like it had pieces of bones in it. By the time they reached the bottom of the walkway, where the bridge met the city, Stella knew exactly where she wanted to go.

"You ready?" she asked Gavin softly, smiling as he nodded curtly in reply.

Stella broke into a sprint that could cause her oxygen pill to erupt in her lungs within minutes. Her feet pounded against the concrete, dashing forward. If any of the infected heard, Stella and Gavin would be gone before they could pinpoint where the noise was coming from.

They had blown past two long blocks of sidewalks before they could even see the infected in the street up ahead. Stella turned to the side and flung the Suicide Prevention Lifeline sign like a Frisbee, hearing a satisfying clang of metal hitting metal, directing the attention of infected up ahead to a spot in the opposite direction. Out of the corner of her eye, she saw the pink and orange of a Dunkin' Donuts surrounded by windows that were intact. She veered sideways into it, pulled open the door, and held it for Gavin to slide in before she followed after him.

Stella dropped to the ground, finding the lock on the bottom of the door and twisting it, shutting out the danger from the outside. She glanced around the room, checking that it was clear, before she leaned heavily against the wall. Her back slid down to the floor as she exhaled heavily.

Her heartbeat thudded loud enough for her to hear it. She forced herself to relax, slowing the racing beat of it.

Gavin sat next to her as her oxygen pill stabilized.

"Are we safe here?" he asked her quietly.

"If they haven't gotten in here after fifteen years, they aren't getting in tonight. Thank God they never got the hang of door handles." Stella pulled off the shirt she had taken from a long-dead infected and threw it into the corner of the room.

Gavin took that as a signal to do the same.

The ache in her muscles intensified—a reminder that they had walked all through the safe hours without stopping. Ignoring the protest in her legs, Stella pushed herself up to her feet. She examined the store, which still hummed with electricity. Thanks to the big push a few years before the outbreak to "go green," most of the stores and shops, in the city especially, ran on sustainable energy sources. Not that going green could help stop the spread of the infection; by then, too much damage had already been done.

Stella walked to the counter, lifted up the divider that separated customers from workers, and stepped through. She checked out the industrial-strength coffee makers, pressing buttons and watching a brown stream of liquid drip out. "Do you like coffee, Gavin?"

"I don't know. Never had it," Gavin replied with a shrug.

"It's expired anyway, like everything else."

"Is it safe to eat?"

"It's generally not recommended, and the quality suffers. Most of it has freezer burn. But people are more likely to die from starving out here than from eating frozen food."

Stella walked away from the coffee machines to the back of the stop, stopping before a metal door about seven feet high. As she opened the door, a blast of cold air billowed past her. The freezer was a walk-in-closet, lined with metal shelves and filled with premade baked goods: ready-to-bake bagels, biscuits, muffins, croissants, eggs, sausage, and flatbread.

"We can take this back," Gavin said.

"No, this is just for us." Stella sighed, wishing that it was that simple. As if all they really had to do for the initiation was find some food and bring it with them to the gang.

"Isn't this why we're here?" Gavin gestured at the frozen stacks of baked goods.

"How would we bring it back?" Stella watched his expression as he realized that they didn't have anything to cart the food away in before she continued. "And how would we bring it back without getting killed once it thaws and the infected smell it on us?" Stella walked into the freezer and grabbed two blueberry muffins and a pumpernickel bagel while Gavin took three everything bagels and a croissant.

"We have three problems right now," Stella said once they had laid the baked goods out to defrost. "We have to find a month's supply of nonperishable food they won't be able to smell. We have to find a way to transport it. And we have to do all that without dying."

"That's more than what Xander said. I didn't know he was expecting all this." Gavin ran a nervous hand through his hair.

Stella sighed, deciding to tell him the truth. "Actually, all that he was expecting was for you to die."

6

"What?" Gavin blurted out before he could stop himself.

Die?

It didn't make any sense. Why feed him and take him in? Why let Stella train him? Or come with him? If it was all for nothing, why do any of it?

It couldn't be. Could it?

But the look on Stella's face spelled out the truth. She looked... drained. Like she had seen this play out too many times before.

"You should be flattered." Stella crossed her arms over her stomach. "He sent you all the way to New York to get rid of you."

"Has he done this before?" Gavin watched Stella slowly nod. "How many people before me?"

"Gavin, we see people die out here all the time." Stella sighed. Her words were weighted with years of loss.

She was here because of him. In a place that she already admitted was a death trap. It was his fault.

"What about you?" Gavin lowered his gaze. Worry

bloomed in his core, his stomach tightening. "What if you get hurt?"

Stella smiled tentatively. "Don't worry about me. I've made it out here for years before I met you. If you want to help me, just focus on keeping yourself alive."

Gavin still didn't like it.

The light of the sun died down, bathing the streets in a golden glow that reflected across glass and metal. A patch of light streamed across the small table where they sat eating their bagels.

What would he have to do to survive? Would he have to kill one of the infected? Gavin had studied their biology. They were barely human anymore. If the essence of humanity was the capacity for love and compassion, once the limbic system and anterior insular cortex rotted away, could one be considered human anymore? If the infected threatened the life of someone he cared about, did that even matter?

Anything could go wrong. What was worse, now he had someone looking out for him. No one had ever risked their life for him; he wouldn't allow it. He had always done things on his own.

And afterwards? If they did manage to get out of this in one piece, would Xander still want him dead?

Gavin picked at his bagel, ripping off little pieces of bread and seeds one at a time to give him something to do. Also, he couldn't stand to eat more than a little at a time. The bread he was used to was fresh and manmade, while this food had the hollow texture of something mass-produced and processed by a machine. He was still eating long after Stella had finished and begun lining up her weapons on a table, inspecting each and loading ammunition.

Stella looked up from her firearms to check up on Gavin. "You'd better finish that soon. They're starting to wake, and we don't want them smelling food in here."

Gavin tossed the rest of the bagel into his mouth, trying not to grimace at the over-refined consistency, or at the way the food was strangely compacted. Pieces of it clung to his teeth and coated the inside of his mouth with residue even after he had swallowed it down.

Outside the glass windows, the New York streets steadily filled with the infected. As the natural light of the sun dimmed, lights flickered on automatically. The air became charged with the mechanical hum of electricity as neon shop signs lit up, announcing that these long-abandoned stores were open. Billboards flashed blinking advertisements for Coca Cola, Yahoo, iPads, Comedy Central, Jersey Boys, Hyundai, Sephora, and others that covered the surrounding buildings and illuminated the growing numbers in the street. They came from everywhere, stepping out of broken stores, climbing down stairwells and out of alleyways to stand together, motionless, in the streets.

Gavin watched through the widow. Stella joined his side, peering at their increasing ranks in silence. He felt the need to do something gnawing away at the inside of him and itching down his limbs. They were all just standing there. There had to be something the two of them could do. Stella had come equipped with explosives and had to have enough to take them out. He wanted to whisper the idea to Stella, but he didn't dare make a sound with so many of them right outside their door.

An infected emerged from a tourist shop next to them, joining the others in the street. This one was male, and scars ran all the way down its distended belly, splitting through patches of hair like cracks in a sidewalk. It was naked, save for some bloodstained strands of khakis that clung listlessly to its body. As its yellow eyes stared blindly down the street, Gavin couldn't look away, filled with the suspicion that this infected had to be about his own age. It was too easy to picture himself there instead, visionless yellow eyes on his own face, and his own features lined with scars and the black of his veins.

At the sound of the strangled bleating of a deer, hundreds of heads snapped to attention. Gavin felt vibrations right through the soles of his feet, an audible rumbling around them as the herd of deer charged past. They weren't like any he had seen before—some with four legs, but most with five or more. Many were striped with scars in a five-slash pattern that suggested they were made by human fingernails—wounds that festered, causing the surrounding skin to rot.

In packs, the infected charged, leaping onto their prey like hyenas determined to kill. Working together, jagged fingernails lashed out, scratching out flesh and hair and, when they made solid contact, holding on. Right in front of their store window, one deer struggled against nine of them. It bellowed and thrashed its antlers about, spearing one in the stomach and adding to the spider web of scars. The infected disentangled itself from the six-tine antlers, spilling more blood onto its tattered khakis, and sank its teeth into the muscles of its prey's neck. The deer let out a scream that rang out until it collapsed.

At the thud of impact, Gavin grabbed Stella, circling his arms around her, protecting her as best as he could. His body was tense and ready to run away and fight if it came to that. There were too many of them. They were just outside the door, and strong enough to break through if they wanted to. The rhythm of her heartbeat drummed so loud

Gavin could feel it against his chest, mirroring his own fast beating.

The body scraped against the concrete as the infected fought over it, snarling as they tore into the deer, which still bleated feebly as the infected ate it alive. Gavin held Stella even after the feeding frenzy ended and the crowd of infected ran off, chasing down other prey. They had finished off more than just flesh, cracking through the skeleton to eat bone and marrow. Gavin couldn't look away from the windows, stunned.

Stella twisted around in his arms so that she faced him, just inches away. She peered into his eyes, carefully reading his expression.

Gavin's arm muscles drew taut and immobile, wondering if he had made a mistake.

Tentatively, she brought her hands up and around his neck so that she was holding him back.

Gavin relaxed into her warm touch, feeling the adrenaline that had spiked in his blood slowing back down again.

She leaned in so that her cheek brushed against his ear as she whispered, "Are you okay?"

At the kind words, Gavin squeezed his eyes shut, relishing the moment. "Yes, I'm fine." He felt like nothing could go wrong when she was here in his arms. Yet, he opened his eyes, looking out the open window into the space where the infected had completed their hunt just minutes before. Out there, it was different. "But there are so many of them."

"It doesn't matter how many of them there are," Stella said, reassuring him. She was whispering, Gavin realized, so as to not attract the attention of the creatures hunting outside. "We can make it; we can do this. So long as we follow the rules." Stella still hadn't moved, and she was closer than she had ever been, her body pressed right against him as she whispered into his ears.

Gavin's heart raced, and all along his arms and the nape of his neck, his hair lifted. The memory of the hunt overshadowed everything. Gavin tightened his arms around her as he listened.

"The first rule of the city is to know where to go. Never go into a store with broken glass. Nothing with automatic sliding doors. You want to look for a place with door handles; that's the kind of store they won't have gotten to already."

Gavin considered all the buildings they had passed on their dash into the Dunkin' Donuts. He just remembered a string of smashed and blood-smeared windows. He was amazed that Stella could even find this place at the pace they were going.

"The second rule of the city is silent kills. You're going to run out of bullets before you run out of the infected. Shooting attracts the attention of every infected in hearing range. So do whatever you can to kill them quietly. Knock them out with a shovel, poison them, spear them. Just get creative," Stella whispered.

Gavin thought back to the bridge, how Stella found a metal sign and turned it into a weapon. There were plenty of dangerous things he could use. In fact, almost anything used the wrong way had the potential to be lethal.

For the last rule, Stella pulled away to look Gavin in the eye. She spoke softly, but Gavin was so tuned into her voice that each word hung in the air as if it carried its own weight. "The third rule of the city," Stella continued, "is to move quickly and get out as fast as you can. The best way to survive is to not be in the city in the first place. But if you are here, get what you need fast and get out."

Stella's violet eyes studied him. After a moment, she sighed. "I meant what I said on the bridge. If we get separated, get out. I don't want anyone to die for me. Especially not you."

He had to look away from her sharp glare as he said in a faint voice, "I don't know if I can promise you that." Gavin could feel Stella's eyes on him, but he couldn't bring himself to raise his eyes to her, afraid that she would be angry.

Finally, Stella said, "Now that they've eaten, they probably won't bother us in the morning." At the change of subject, Gavin peered back up at her nervously to find an amused look on her face. "You should try to get some sleep."

Stella disentangled herself from Gavin's hold and walked back without another word to the table where she had arranged her weapons and ammunition.

How could anyone sleep after seeing the horde? Eventually, he eased himself into a comfortable position and followed Stella's advice.

"HEY, WAKE UP," STELLA WHISPERED.

Gavin jolted awake. The dream had seemed so real. He tried to remember—it had seemed important. He was home, back in the largest dome of the oxygen factory. The images were getting jumbled up now, but he could recall the rows of luminescent kelp. As he bent over one strand to take a sample, he remembered seeing a reflection, a familiar face.

"Come on." Stella's voice cut through his reverie. "They've started to fall asleep now. If we move quietly, it should be safe out there."

Reality descended on his mind like night settling in at the turn of day. It was to be their first day scavenging. Gavin was going to be among deadly monsters and guided by the most beautiful woman he had ever seen.

Gavin dipped his head to hide the flush of red in his cheeks and neck.

"Eat this quick." Stella handed him an everything bagel while she packed a handful of extra food into her bag.

To distract himself from the taste of the bagel, Gavin thought back to the other women he had come across. There were a handful of girls back at the factory, some that were even his age. Not that he really noticed them; he was usually focused on work. Then there were the women in pictures and movies from the old age that the original scientists thought to bring with them in their mad scramble to escape infection. There were all the women that he had seen in his twenty years of life. Then there was Stella.

As an albino, she was unique. Every one of her features was delicate. Her pale skin contrasted all the colors all around them—the pink and orange of the Dunkin' Donuts, the brown of the wood, the black of the countertop. Stella simply seemed unearthly, like she couldn't possibly belong here. The first time he saw her, he had thought he was dead and Stella was an angel. Except that angels couldn't be as warm as Stella when she placed her fingers lightly on his chin, staring intently at him.

Despite her dainty appearance, Stella was a match for anything out there. He frowned. Gavin had to learn how to deal with the infected to be of some use to her. Back at the factory, he could take down a full-grown bull, or track down and tranquilize a leopard. He just needed to adapt to life out here. He would remember the rules.

Stella knelt before the front door, clenching her eyes shut for a moment, lost in thought. Next, her hand shot out to the bottom door latch, turning the lock. She pulled the door toward her, peering out into the street until she was satisfied that their path was clear. They walked through the door, shutting it behind them without a sound. Stella used the grime-coated shirts from the day before to wipe the door down. To hide their smell.

The streets had a different look to them, now that Gavin was aware of exactly the kind of creatures that lived within. As he followed Stella down the streets, he was wary of each of his footfalls. He carefully stepped around the bits of debris, trying to watch everything at once. He tried to step silently around soda cans and plastic heaps, not sure how to avoid noise. All the while, he was attempting to look about him, keeping in mind every single one of those signs of the infected. He tried to recall word for word Stella's warnings about the infected. Look around and be aware of everything that could be used as a weapon. Look for places with door handles; the infected couldn't figure out how to use them. Get far away from anything made of broken glass. Don't go into the sensor of those sliding doors. Don't step on that garbage. Don't make a noise.

Stella was quietly observing the way he tried and failed to watch everything. Calmly, Stella slowed her pace to match his own. She slipped her fingers around his, squeezing them reassuringly.

They walked hand in hand one block away from the Dunkin' Donuts, and Gavin estimated that it would only take them ten minutes to go back to the bridge from here. They could do that easily enough if there was nothing chasing them. They crossed another street, and then a few blocks more, each step taking them farther away from relative safety. Gavin watched Stella for clues. Stella just strode with a naturally silent step. She moved confidently, without looking every which way like he had.

What did she think of him? Yes, she was holding his hand, and she had gone out of her way to save his life, but what if that was something she would do for anybody?

Stella broke the silence, startling him. "We have to be quiet, but we don't have to be silent right now," Stella spoke in such a low voice that Gavin had to strain to hear her. "They hunted well last night. We were lucky the herd was here. So most of them should be asleep."

Gavin didn't trust himself to reply. What if he couldn't speak softly enough?

Stella didn't seem to mind his silence. After a pause, she let him in on her plan. "I know a place that should have what we're looking for. We can try there first."

This place ended up being a small restaurant with a sleek black awning still labeled as "Carmines". At first glance, the building looked similar to its neighbors, until Gavin noticed the reinforced glass windows and the old-fashioned round doorknobs that would cause the infected some trouble.

Stella twisted the doorknob and pushed the heavy brass door forward. Like many of the other buildings in the area, the renewable resources still functioned, and the room still had electricity. However, the restaurant sought a romantic atmosphere with dim light. The silver candelabras had long gone out, leaving behind melted remains. Most of the lighting came from a chandelier, with its pen shell shades casting the room in honey-colored hues.

In the limited visibility, Gavin could make out tables covered in burgundy cloths. On those tables lay porcelain plates and crystal wine glasses, undisturbed for the last decade and a half. Some plates were covered with the residue of food that had long since rotted away.

Besides some broken glasses and overturned chairs, the

restaurant seemed peaceful. It reminded Gavin of pictures of the old days he had seen, with men in suits enjoying fine dining with women in cocktail dresses. It was a strange testament that the world was once normal.

Gavin followed Stella across the dining area and to the back, where she pushed her way through swinging double doors. The room was filled with stainless steel appliances. Buzzing fluorescent lights shone off the clean chrome blenders, mixers, toasters, and coffee pots. There was a huge sink stacked with dirty dishes and metal trays that were never going to be washed. They walked by the rows of stoves, passing through the kitchen without a second glance. Stella headed for a wooden door, which looked out of place surrounded by all the metal. She placed her palm flat on the door and pushed it open cautiously, revealing a narrow stairway.

The wooden staircase was layered with a thick coating of dust. Stella reached one hand out to each side of the brick walls to brace herself as she carefully lowered one foot to the first step. Despite the care she took, the staircase let out an aching squeak. They froze at the sound. Waiting. But nothing reacted to the noise. It seemed that they were clear for the moment. Stella placed her fingers against the brick wall, locking into the hollow of the mortar, her arms taking most of her weight.

Again, Gavin watched as Stella eased her foot onto the rickety wooden staircase. The aged wood responded with a softer creak, like a sigh. Stella let go of her hold on the wall, reaching lower. Bracing herself against the crumbling brick walls, she maneuvered her way down.

Gavin heard another faint creak farther down the stairs as Stella moved on.

He hesitated by the wall, holding the door open to

provide the room with a source of light; the incandescent bulb hanging above the stairwell had burnt out long ago. He wondered whether he should stay or follow. He doubted the wood would be able to support his weight, but Stella had trudged along, getting further and further away, almost disappearing into the dark. There was no way he was going to let her go off alone. Once Stella was more than halfway down the staircase, Gavin took one step deeper into the room. He let the light source shut off behind them, casting them into darkness. From an inner pocket, he pulled out a high-powered light-emitting diode and clicked it on. It let out a focused ring of light directly in front of him, casting a halo around Stella.

Gavin followed Stella, ignoring the wooden stairway completely. Instead, he braced his hands and feet on each side of the wall, shimmying his way down, holding his body just above the staircase without ever touching the wood.

Stella reached the bottom before him, out of the range of Gavin's light. Gavin was alone with just a tiny circle of visibility in the darkness. He could do better than this. Gavin swung forward, shooting down the remaining steps, catching himself on the wall with just the small scrape of his hands against crumbling brick and mortar. He released his hold on the wall, stepping down to the basement floor.

He was alone, with a small patch of light and darkness all around, in a place he didn't know. Sweeping the light in an arc, he looked for Stella. It wasn't as if he could call out her name and put them in danger. His limited light shone on the shelves of a pantry, mostly filled with boxes chewed through by rats.

He couldn't see her anywhere. Flashing his light in every direction showed nothing but the garbage-strewn shelves of the pantry.

Panic flooded through him, breaking his concentration and his better judgment. Gavin shook his head. Stressing himself out looking for each and every sign of danger wasn't helping.

In fight or flight mode, blood pressure raised, he couldn't think. All he could hear was the adrenaline pumping through his body, his heart drumming, and the oxygen pill ticking from deep within his chest.

This nervous, he wasn't a help to anyone at all.

Gavin forced himself to close his eyes for a moment to listen, just listen. His mind automatically separated the noises that he knew were important from those that were not. He heard the hum of electricity, the idle ticking of something like a carbon monoxide alarm. In the distance there was the faint dripping of water. He also caught a sound that was familiar, like the gentle rush of the wind, except that it was too steady. Too regular. Almost like breathing.

Gavin tensed all the muscles in his jaw and clenched his fists so tight he could feel his nails biting into skin. It was too loud to be an animal. Now that he had noticed the breaths, he couldn't get them out of his mind. All the relaxation he had coaxed into his system was gone. He had to find Stella.

He wasn't used to sifting through noises, instead choosing to ignore them as much as possible in the factory. But he recognized the feeling of being hunted. Not all of the dangerous animals he worked with would react as soon as they knew you were there.

Working with large predators, like the leopards and wolves, he developed a sense of when he was safe and when he was not. There was a subtle change in the air, a slight twist between the monotonous daily life and that realization that something was about to go terribly wrong. A bull would just charge at a threat, but then there were the more effective predators. The ones that watched, waiting until they had you right where they wanted you. Those were the encounters that usually ended up as close calls, or worse. Exactly what Gavin was facing now.

Something didn't feel right. The muscles in his legs tightened, ready to run. His grip was so tight, the ring of light trembled. Should he call out her name, even though it was against the rules? But then he heard a faint scrape, as if something was removed from a shelf. Gavin pinpointed the location in his mind and walked toward it.

There she was. The tiny light was filled with her outline just a few feet away. She was standing in front of a shelf, examining cans. Gavin stepped toward her, a portion of his panic melting away. At the very least, he knew where she was. She was safe.

Stella quirked her lips into a half smile as he approached. The smile on her face froze when she took in his expression. Her brow furrowed as her eyes darted across their surroundings. Gavin hoped he was wrong. Nothing was out there but his own paranoia.

Her lovely violet eyes widened.

As if compelled, without a choice in the world, Gavin pointed the light in the direction Stella was looking.

Standing there was an infected. It was male, with long strands of greasy hair that grew all the way to its naked chest, half covering solid yellow eyes that directed their blind gaze straight at Stella. The quiet wheeze of air moved in and out of the infected's open mouth.

Gavin turned the light back on Stella, who glared at Gavin with a fierce look. She pointed straight ahead, back at the stairway, their only source of safety.

It was an order. One that went against every fiber of his

conscience. How could she expect him to back away from danger and to leave her here with it? There might be more of them waiting out in the dark.

He wanted to argue, but he didn't dare waste her time. Not now. Stella must have a plan. He stepped backward toward the stairway, keeping his eyes on Stella and the infected the entire time, ready to jump back and help at a moment's notice. This was dangerous.

Gavin recalled his first lesson about the infected. His brother's words echoed in his mind. *If they bite you, they will infect you. Toxins will surge through your blood until you become like them. Or until you die.*

No.

Gavin couldn't let that happen. He couldn't let her come to harm. Not because of him.

Bracing himself against the walls of the stairs, Gavin held the light with his teeth. He stepped down without taking his eyes off either the infected or Stella, listening to the soft creak of his foot against the stairs.

Neither Stella nor the infected paid him any attention. Both stood frozen, their attention locked on one another.

Once he was too high to keep the light pointed on them, Gavin paused, swallowing down the dry sensation in his throat. Stella had more experience with all of this; he had to trust her. Gavin eased himself up one more step, watching the light raise higher until he couldn't see Stella or the infected at all.

All he saw was the movement at the edge of the light when Stella ran farther into the pantry as the infected shrieked its hunting call and charged after her. Gavin took a step back down, turning the flashlight about, looking after them, but the two of them were already deeper in the darkness.

Gavin hesitated. What if he made a bad situation worse? That indecision vanished when he heard the answering cry to the infected's hunting call. More were joining in the hunt.

Gavin thought back to the survival rules as he dashed up the stairs, not even caring if he made noise. First rule, know where to go. Gavin ran into the kitchen, squinting as the full fluorescent lights blinded him.

Second rule, silent kills. As soon as his eyes adjusted to the light, Gavin searched for a weapon—a knife would be perfect. There had to be one somewhere. He opened up empty drawers and felt the pressure of the time slipping away. Any second could be Stella's last. He grabbed a carbon-steel frying pan off a drying rack.

Third rule, move quickly and get out fast. Gavin ran back toward the staircase and down the rickety old stairs.

Holding the frying pan high in one hand, Gavin swerved the light through the pitch black with the other. He listened for her, hearing nothing. Gavin was painfully aware of every footstep, the rustle of his clothing as he moved. The lack of sounds from other living creatures. It was as if he was alone. What was he missing? What he was doing wrong?

I'm thinking like the prey, not the predator.

He was too nervous. Gavin clenched his grip on the frying pan, reassuring himself. Even though he'd never done this before, he had advantages that they did not. He had his vision, and his mental faculties.

Gavin followed the direction he had seen Stella run. The infected might be hunters, but Gavin was no weakling either. He made his way further into the pantry, passing shelves stocked with what used to be ingredients for fine dining cuisine but were now the crumbling food of rats.

It wasn't long before he heard the sound of breathing again.

This time the breaths were labored, like someone taking in air after chasing something. Gavin's flashlight showed three of them. The first infected was joined by an elderly male who had white tufts of a beard darkened with food stains, and a shorter female who couldn't keep still. Her outstretched fingers twitched like a cat flexing its claws.

The three surrounded Stella, who was standing perfectly still. She broke her motionless stance, turning her head toward Gavin, her eyes wide with surprise. The male charged at Stella, who turned and leaped just as quickly. One of the infected's fingernails snagged against the nylon of her backpack, locking on.

Stella's momentum caused her to lurch forward, dragging the infected right along with her. Automatically, she slipped off the backpack, putting space between her and the danger. As the creature tore into the bag, Stella got three steps away before she came to a jarring stop, her feet scraping to a halt against the concrete basement floor. She turned, staring at the infected male as he tore the nylon fabric of the backpack apart, spilling the contents onto the floor.

The creature ripped into the bag, eating bagel and nylon fabric both. Now clear, Stella could make a run for it. They could regroup and try someplace new. But Stella wasn't moving.

What was she doing?

Hands curling like talons were the only warning the female infected gave before it charged.

Gavin intercepted, knocking it off balance before slamming the frying pan down hard on its forehead. It dropped to the ground, still.

One down, two to go.

The older infected tasted the air, tongue lolling, as

sludge-like saliva trickled down into its beard. Its attention was fixed on Stella.

Gavin raised his frying pan high and at the ready, freezing at the quick double bang of gunfire.

She'd taken out the last two cleanly with bullets to the head. Their bodies collapsed to the ground as the reverberations of gunfire echoed in Gavin's ear after the long silence of the basement cellar. A tremor ran down his spine and fear crawled up his sides. Stella had just broken her own rule. She had to have a good reason for that.

Rummaging through the tattered remains of her bag, Stella ignored the rounds of ammunition spilled across the floor, and she pushed two handguns off to the side. Gavin kept the light on the mess, hoping to help out. Her face was a picture of fierce determination illuminated in the gloom as she picked through the saliva-coated disorder. For the past two nights, she had lined up all the contents of the bag. What was in there that was so important? It wasn't safe here.

Then Gavin heard it—indistinct at first, but getting louder and more defined by the second. It took him a second to figure out what that dull pounding meant. He was listening to bare feet slapping against concrete.

"Stella, do you hear that? We have to get out of here," Gavin said quietly, searching for the source of the sound. The restaurant entranceway on the first floor was undisturbed; they had to have gotten in from the basement. If three infected had done it once, others could do it again. By the sound of it, those shots had woken up more of them. Many more.

Gavin tore his eyes away from the footsteps echoing around in the darkness to look back at Stella. She was shifting through the items in the bag quickly now. She gave no signs of having heard either Gavin or the approaching footsteps.

"Stella, we have to get out of here," Gavin tried again. He had no idea what she was doing, but it didn't matter. They were out of time. The footsteps were too clear now. They had let them get too close.

With the experience of all the years working the hard jobs no one else wanted, everything from draining abscesses on skittish one-ton horses to taking down the 2,800-pound bulls for castration and rounding up the full-grown boars to slaughter and disembowel them, Gavin slipped behind Stella and grabbed her under the arms, yanking her away from the remnants of her bag.

Stella fought to get back, twisting against his hold to wrench her way free. She moved with silent ferocity, grappling and kicking out against his grip. Gavin held her as he ran back to the staircase and up the stairs, regretting each loud creak that left behind a trail of breadcrumbs for the infected to follow.

Gavin turned around when he got to the top of the stairs, swinging the door to the kitchens open. The high-powered industrial lights lit up the basement enough to show the events that were unfolding behind them. The shots had attracted a mob of the infected. They were streaming in. There must have been a hole in the wall where old brick had crumbled or the wooden barricade had rotted away. They converged around Stella's bag, some ripping into the scattered materials, shoving anything into their mouths that looked edible, while others surrounded the bodies of the fallen infected. Gavin tensed at the sight of the horde eating their own dead.

The infected at the edge, jostled and pushed away from the food, stopped and straightened. The nearest infected male pointed its nose up in the air, stretching out onto the tips of its toes and pivoting, until it faced the source of a new smell—the direction of the stairway.

Gavin had seen enough. He slammed the door shut, bracing against the wood. Moments later, the infected hammered against the door from the basement side.

"Let me go." Stella tensed in Gavin's arms, swallowing nervously. "We have to hurry."

Gavin released his hold and Stella ran off. Gavin braced both of his arms against the door as the infected slammed against it. He didn't know how many were behind the door. The flimsy old wood wasn't going to hold out for long.

Gavin almost didn't notice the sound of something heavy rolling across the epoxy flooring until Stella came back into view, pushing an industrial kitchen island. Gavin backed away, allowing the heavy wooden structure to take his place.

Stella fastened down the wheel locks, immobilizing the metal cart. She snatched Gavin's hand in her own. "Let's go."

She sprinted out of the kitchens, bursting through the double doors. The two of them were halfway through the dining area, crossing through the rows of tables, when they heard the blasts.

Three explosions, one after another. Gavin felt the vibrations straight through the soles of his boots.

Stella slowed to a halt, gritting her teeth. "They got to the grenades."

"That's what you were looking for?" Gavin asked.

Stella nodded, swallowing heavily. "That's going to wake them up. It's going to wake them all up, for miles in every direction."

Gavin could imagine them, all of them, stretching from their sleep and opening up their blind eyes. He pictured them coming out of broken-down stores, crawling out of smashed windows. Every one of them had just been invited to the hunt. Here he and Stella still stood, mere moments from the blast site, their new fresh prey.

"Run!" Stella cried.

7

I t was stupid of Stella to come back here.

The city held too many memories for her. She'd gone to this restaurant too many times, back when she'd lived here. Back when things were different—the last time she had ever felt safe. The layout was familiar, almost comforting. But memories were a distraction from reality. She never should have come back.

Stella and Gavin burst out of Carmine's and into the street. They were alone for now, but not for long.

The infected had gotten her bag, filled with all their food rations and most of the weapons. She hadn't wanted to put Gavin at risk and assumed she'd be better prepared to defend the supplies.

Now the grenade blasts were a wake-up call to the hundreds of thousands of infected in the city. It no longer mattered if they were well fed, or that they were in the safe hours.

The infected were coming. All of them.

Even now, the first of them stepped out of buildings, cautiously making their way out into the sun. She and Gavin ran past one that yawned wide, showing teeth chipped into points and browned, as it rubbed at sightless eyes. With the infected awakened, when they needed it the most, they had less than half of their supplies.

"The bridge is the other way," Gavin panted out as they took off, straight in the middle of the street.

He was right; the George Washington Bridge had to be their best bet for safety. The two of them could just leave the city, find safety for the night, and try again tomorrow. The muscles in her legs were screaming with strain, and she didn't even want to think about what this run was doing to her oxygen pill. Even at the pace they were going, there was no way they could outrun all the infected—they would either be taken down en route, or while they were running across the bridge.

"We aren't going to make it back to the bridge," Stella replied. "Look for a bank. TD, Bank of America, Citi, Wells Fargo, Chase. They've got reinforced glass windows."

The buildings lining the street had fading words on awnings and half-destroyed signs. Gavin had probably never seen a bank before, but it was something to focus on besides the infected stepping out into the open all around them.

Most of the infected wandered toward the sound of the blast. If enough of the creatures died in the explosion, it would feed the others, distracting them. However, some of those newly woken heads turned in the direction of their footsteps.

The Chase bank was sturdy enough and three blocks away. If they could make it there.

Somewhere behind them, Stella heard one of the infected let out a hunting cry. Adrenaline rushed through her as she realized that they had run out of time. Footsteps shadowed their own.

Stella had seen firsthand the aftermath when a pack of infected hunted for humans. More than once she had seen the chase, the desperation of the victims. They screamed out for help, unwittingly attracting more, like flies to honey. Every time Stella had seen this, from when she was a toddler peering out windows at her father's side, to now with the infected running at her back, she always made the same vow. That wasn't going to happen to her.

Abruptly, Stella cut sideways and down a street.

Gavin pivoted, throwing off the infected just behind him. The infected mob chasing them was cut in half—one group blindly continued down the main road, while the others ran down 173rd Street after them.

Stella ran to the steel-framed door of a brick building, under the placard "Fresh Meadow School." She tugged the handle of the door, but it was locked. She slashed her dagger against her palm, making a small cut, and smeared it against the metal. She clenched her fist, hiding the scent of blood on her, as she turned and leaped down the stairs.

While running, she listened. Behind them, another group of the infected broke off from the rest of the hunt, distracted by the scent of fresh blood. They smacked and tore against the door, mindlessly attempting to break in.

She had thrown off some, but not enough of them.

They needed shelter. Anything. The surrounding buildings had broken glass and doors ripped off hinges. In between a row of cars with smashed windows sat a van. Stella veered straight toward it. She pulled open the back double-door of the van, revealing boxes stacked high.

"Get in." Stella watched Gavin clamber into the tight space before leaping in after him. She reached down—as the horde ran straight after them with their arms outstretched and their mouths opened wide—and slammed the door shut.

The infected crashed into the van. The force of their collision dented the metal and jostled everything inside. All around them, the metal screeched as the infected grated at their enclosure with nails and teeth. Their hunting bellows mixed in with frustrated screams and fists pounding.

Stella pulled her Glock from its holster, locking it into position. She stared down the sight of the barrel, her finger on the trigger.

Stella lay on top of the boxes, poised and ready.

If any of the infected managed to snag its hand on the handle, exposing them, if one ripped through the metal, she was their last line of defense.

There were too many of them, but it might be enough to give Gavin a chance to escape.

If this was the end of her, so be it. She'd watched so many others die already.

The attack slowed down.

After ten minutes, the majority of them drifted away. Maybe to turn back to their broken buildings to go back to sleep, or to find an easier meal.

Stella kept her hand ready on the trigger. Ten minutes turned into twenty, then twenty-five, and Stella still did not take her eyes away from the back of the van. She waited, even after the sounds of attack disintegrated into silence. The minutes stretched on, and Stella did not waver. Not to wipe the sweat off her brows and out of her eyes. Not to reposition herself on the boxes, even as hard edges pressed against her. From outside the van came the frustrated snort and the soft pad of footsteps as the last infected left them. Finally, she lowered the gun and exhaled a sigh of relief.

Gavin watched her, frowning. She whispered to him, "What is it?"

"What were you looking for in your bag, besides the grenades?"

The question surprised her. They had just been chased by hundreds of the infected. Today was the closest Stella had gotten to death in years. She had gone through worse encounters, but never with so many, when so much could have gone wrong.

"Nothing that can hurt us now," Stella said. There were no more explosives to bring all the infected denizens of New York down upon them. What she lost was nothing like that.

"But it was important?" Gavin asked.

"Just to me," Stella said simply.

His gray eyes were soft with concern. Gavin's worry filled Stella with guilt. Compared to their lives, to their safety, she hadn't lost much.

"What was it?" Gavin asked.

Stella paused.

Would he understand? People didn't tend to ask her personal questions. None of the others in her gang, not even her close friends Xander and Sam, would fight for what she lost today. Neither of them would agree that it was worth it. Stella suspected that Gavin would; he wasn't anything like the others.

"A picture of my parents," Stella sighed. "It was all I had left of them."

She had lost them all over again. Never to see their faces again. How long did she have until her memories of them faded completely? Grief settled over her heart like a well-worn cloak.

Surrounded by abandoned houses, filled with pearls, diamonds and trinkets which fetched high prices underground, that picture had been her only possession of any value. For as long as she lived, every day the infected were going to attack her. She would have plenty of opportunities to be killed by them. But all that remained of her mother and her father was one four-by-six-inch photograph. Now it was gone.

Xander would call it another distraction, and he was right. Stella had thought of the pictures first, before remembering herself and searching for the explosives.

"Also," Stella added, wanting Gavin to know what they were up against, "there was the ammunition. More than half was lost with my bag. It's tough enough surviving with ammo and now we don't have enough."

"I'm sorry," Gavin whispered. "If I hadn't pulled you out of that basement, we'd have the ammunition and you'd have that photo."

Stella shook her head. He was overestimating her. "What are you talking about? If you hadn't gotten me out of there, I would have been eaten."

Gavin held his face in his hand, looking at the dents in the van. The brief moment of confidence Gavin had shown in the basement was gone. Why did he look so uncertain? He needed to trust himself.

"Look at me." Stella waited until those gray eyes nervously met her own. "You trusted your instincts there, and you saved my life. I don't know why you doubt yourself. I will never come back to this city again. Never. Unless it's with you. I wouldn't want anyone else beside me."

Stella was suddenly aware of how close Gavin was. She couldn't help but look down at his lips, wondering what they would taste like.

She blinked. Where had that thought come from? She definitely wasn't in the habit of kissing handsome men in the back of vans, surrounded by creatures that wanted to kill her. She looked away from Gavin's mouth, stopping herself. Things had gotten bad enough already without Stella finding a new way to distract them.

"Let's see if it's safe to leave the van," Stella said, getting herself back on track. She looked for the exit in the dim light of the windowless vehicle. Light streamed through the perforated van partition that separated the cargo in the back from the passenger section in the front. Stella looked through the holes of the partition, taking in the gruesome sight of what lay on the other side. She had no choice. There was no other exit. She unlatched the partition and slid it open.

In the front of the van sat two bodies. Even decayed as they were, Stella could clearly see the holes in their foreheads where gunfire had ended both of their lives. Brown splatters were crusted into the suede car seats, the vinyl door panels, the console, and over the dashboard. Even soiled, Stella could recognize the uniforms on the corpses. They were wearing the standard worker's uniform from the underground city.

The uniforms gave Stella an idea. She turned back to the cargo hold and opened one of the boxes. It was packed tight, full of cans. Stella picked up one of the cans, reading the Campbell's Chunky Classic Chicken Noodle label.

"Looks like these two did our work for us," Stella said grimly. "We might have gotten away with bringing back just one of these boxes." She pulled out another can of Del Monte Fresh Cut Sweet Peas and said, "There's even vegetables here for you. Now you won't have to starve."

"What happened to them?" Gavin asked, causing Stella to give the two another look over. For years she'd seen bodies out in the desert. It was just a fact of existence that not everyone lived. Even in the underground, if she stumbled across a pair of bodies, she wouldn't question it. But for Gavin, death just wasn't normal.

"The bodies are about two weeks gone." Stella suppressed memories of how she became so acquainted with the length of decay. "They were from the underground at some point. These clothes are for maintenance. Both of them were shot, and they did it to themselves." Noticing Gavin's look of surprise, she added, "The infected can't use guns. Even if their brains could process how it works, they wouldn't be able to see targets anyway."

"Why would these men do something like that?" Gavin asked.

"One of them probably got infected. He didn't want to believe it and tried to hide it. Once the infection traveled into his brain, he attacked his partner." Stella pointed to the corpse in the driver's seat who was closest to the handgun. "The partner here must have gotten bit before he managed to shoot. He knew what was coming. Chose to end it himself."

"What were they doing out of the underground city anyway? If they were still in the human establishment, this wouldn't have happened," Gavin said.

Stella shook her head, saying nothing. He was wrong of course about how things happened underground, but that was a conversation for another time. Gavin was upset enough by these deaths already.

"They must have escaped," Stella said. "They had to have gone to Celia's gang, since I haven't heard about these two. They probably came here for an initiation. Things just didn't end well for them."

Gavin had gone quiet. Stella waited for a moment to see if he would have anything else to say. But only just a moment. Now that she had been given a way out of the city, she was going to take it.

"Let's see if we can finish their last job," Stella mused. She routed through the dead man's pockets, fishing out a set of car keys. She leaned over the body to fit the key into the ignition. One quick glance told her that they were alone. She twisted the key, heard a click, click, click, and then nothing.

Stella tried again, listening to the clicking, waiting for the hum of the engine springing to life. Instead, there was more silence. Stella switched the car back off and leaned against the headrest. "After waking up every infected in the city and getting chased by half of them, it would have been too easy if this van would just start and we could drive it back," she muttered, wondering if there was a way to salvage the situation.

"Maybe I can fix it," Gavin said.

Stella lifted a brow. "All right, I'll cover you."

Could this vehicle even be fixed, or were they just wasting time? She had looked under the hood of a car before and found a maze of wires and metal as intricate as the pathways in the underground city. Unlike the city, she had no way of knowing how everything connected together.

"Leave him in here," Stella cautioned as she saw Gavin open the passenger door and almost let one of the bodies drop to the ground outside. "We don't want to advertise that we're here." Gavin stepped over the body gingerly and Stella followed, pulling out her Glock and casting a look around. Now that the infected had been woken up and given a chase, there was no telling what they would do.

Gavin lifted the hood of the van with a creak, looking inside. His fingers traced the pathways of wires and metal. Had he ever even seen an automobile engine before? What was the use of a car at the bottom of the ocean, and how would those scientists even manage to get one there?

Stella scanned their surroundings. Her gaze passed over the locked school building doors and flicked to the hollow, burnt-out husks of trees. She scanned the dusty streets and sidewalks, which were empty for now.

She heard the faint clang and jangle from under the hood, the rustle of the wind, and from deep inside her lungs she heard a warning chime that resonated all the way to her ears. Her oxygen pill would stop working in exactly five minutes. She started to reach for her inner pockets where she kept her pill stash, but she stopped herself. Gavin was distracted right now; he wouldn't notice.

Every thirty seconds, Stella heard the ping. She ignored it, concentrating instead on the unchanging landscape as she looked for signs of trouble. Then the pings stopped, and Stella felt a pressure in her lungs and an ache in her nose and throat that let her know that the pill was finished.

The smells came in a rush. At first, she couldn't sort out what was what. First the smell of the decaying bodies over-powered everything else. Stella stepped away from the van inconspicuously, controlling and smoothing out her features. She stopped the gag, which would have given her away. When the smell of decomposing flesh faded, Stella picked up the scents of the city, like urine, asphalt, and the rot of thousands of ransacked buildings and apartments that had been exposed to the elements.

Then there was that lingering smell that coated every-thing, that chemical smell that was almost sweet and reminded Stella of Fantastik Citrus spray. It was the smell of the infection in the open air, and the infected reeked of it.

After checking to see that Gavin was still busy, Stella inhaled a deep breath. She concentrated as if she had gone days without eating and had to smell out a source of food. She could smell where that chemical lemon scent was the most concentrated. Her eyes trailed to the spot where her nose told her that the infected hid, and she found herself looking upon a broken window in the lower level of the school. So the infected hadn't left. They would just have to be careful, then, not to attract their attention.

"I think it should work now." Gavin closed the hood.

Stella winced when she heard the sharp click as the rusted metal latched back into place.

"It's a hybrid engine with an internal combustion chamber. The spark plug wasn't igniting," Gavin said.

"All right, start her up," Stella motioned for Gavin to get moving, trying to get him back into safety, as she glanced at the broken school window. She wasn't about to give up now, not when the two of them were so close to escape. Not when the infected had already destroyed that last photo, all she had left of fading memories.

She ignored the gust of concentrated rotten air as Gavin re-entered the van. She was sure that if the infected were awake, that smell alone would seize their attention. The keys clinked as Gavin fumbled to start the ignition. Without taking her eyes off the infected's hideaway, she listened. The engine churned with a loud rickety clacking, followed by a deep, throaty rumble as it started up.

Stella was glad that she was facing the brick building and that Gavin couldn't see the amused smirk on her face. The part of her that wondered just how good of a mechanic Gavin was just got an answer. The two of them had accomplished what they set off to do somehow. Though things weren't over yet.

A pale human outline emerged from the darkness of the

window. The infected human made subtle movements as it tested the air outside.

She had time to walk back to the van and start driving away, but opening the van would flood the air with the pungent odor of rotting meat. It could drive the infected into a frenzy. Stella imagined the infected chasing them down the street, breaking through the windshield and clawing at them.

She wasn't going to take any chances.

She reached into the leather sheath at her side, pulling out her dagger. Pressing her thumb against the sharpened steel edge, she moved. Her worn leather shoes eased soundlessly against the asphalt as she crept up to the brick building.

The infected's sunburned face pointed toward the van, wide nostrils flaring. A four-fingered hand clenched onto the cement of the windowsill. From her angle, she could only see the one infected as it focused on the running engine. She angled herself carefully, waiting.

When the infected sprung out from the windowsill, Stella sprung too. She kicked the legs out from under it and leaped on its back, slamming it against the sidewalk with their combined weight. Before the creature could right itself and retaliate, Stella sunk her dagger into its neck and twisted it.

With her swift attack, Stella wasn't expecting the infected to buck her off, but after one powerful jolt, she was knocked off sideways. She pushed herself up and leaped away, putting as much space in between the two of them as she could. The creature righted itself, getting back to its feet. The blood dripping from its neck didn't slow it down at all.

She cursed inwardly as the creature stared straight through the space between them to where she stood, tracing the soft sounds she made as she caught her breath. Without her pill, she was a lot more aware of where the infected hid, but they were also more aware of her.

There was nowhere for her to hide, and she had already used up her chance to surprise it. This infected was stronger than average, perhaps even stronger than her. Stella's hand itched as she stared at her weapon, still lodged in the creature's neck. That weapon was her best chance of taking the infected out quietly. She cast her eyes about, looking for an alternative.

In an instant, her gaze swept across the dusty cracked pavement, past rusted down cars, past downed traffic lights, settling on a signpost with an arrow indicating that the electric vehicle charging station was to the right. She stamped her feet loud against the asphalt to draw attention to the sound and ran hard. She sprinted without restraint, drawing on the open air in deep breaths, letting it fill her lungs, letting her heart pound without fear.

Stella aimed straight for the signpost, leaping out of the way of the steel metal when she was just an inch away. She heard the thud behind her as the infected charged into the post. Stella spun around to look at the creature.

The metal had pierced straight into rotten skin at the junction of its neck and shoulder. The creature howled, clawing at the air until its hands landed on the steel frame of the sign. It pressed against the steel, pushing its body out until it was completely free. The creature was breathing heavily as it stepped around the post, and its head snapped in the direction Stella was standing.

Stella didn't care if she woke up every infected in the city. She plunged her hand into her holster and got a firm grip on her Glock. Something in her gut told her that if she wanted to stay alive, this creature would soon have to die.

Stella fired. Her fingers were still clenched against the trigger when the bullet soared harmlessly over the infected as it ducked and charged at her. It was too close—close enough to see a web of blackened veins twisted under the rotted skin. She took careful aim, knowing she wouldn't miss again.

The bullet hit the creature square in the jaw, blasting away flesh and teeth. The impact didn't slow it down. Stella had just one moment free to stare at the creature in disbelief, and then its teeth were on her.

A flash of decayed enamel clenched down on her upper arm, impossibly strong. Stella felt the bite all the way down to her bone as the teeth tore into skin and muscle. The sludge-like blood dripped from the infected's bullet wound in fat globs down to her arm, where it could mix with her own blood. The infected's dank yellow eyes widened at the thrill of her taste.

Stella was shaking, barely in control, as her skin turned clammy and her pulse raced. She eased her good arm close to the Glock and, moving it as little as possible, switched the weapon into her free arm. She had to pull herself together before the infected could saw through her flesh and take a chunk out of her.

Large tanned hands appeared at its forehead and chin, straining to wrench the infected off her. Stella's body was numb, and it took her a moment to realize that the hands belonged to Gavin. She struggled through the pain, needing to warn Gavin not to do what he was trying to do. She had to tell him that it was too dangerous, that after the infected bit their teeth into something, they didn't let go. That was before she felt the pressure on her arm ease off.

A little at a time, the teeth loosened, until Gavin completely pried the infected off her. Gavin shoved it hard to the ground a few feet away. Before the infected could scramble back to its feet, Gavin had pulled out his handgun and shot it right in the forehead. Brown sludge trickled from the wound and fell across the infected's dead eyes like tears as the creature moved no more.

Stella stared at Gavin, who still held the gun in his hand. Quietly, she asked him, "Are you going to finish me off?"

"Not if I don't have to," Gavin replied without missing a beat. His answer was too confident, without even a trace of hesitation.

Stella waited for Gavin to break the façade and turn on her, finishing what the infected had started.

Instead, he slipped his drawstring bag down his shoulder and pulled out a bottle of iodine. Stella watched warily as Gavin poured iodine over her forearm. His reaction to her bite was... unexpected. Everyone knew what happened to people who were bitten by the infected, but he didn't even seem nervous.

As Gavin coiled gauze from the medical kit around her injury, Stella relaxed. She leaned her head into his solid presence, allowing him to help her, confident that Gavin wasn't acting or plotting anything against her.

"How did you know?" Stella asked. It wasn't surprising that Gavin had managed to see through her secret, just that it had only taken him three days. Others could spend years around her and never find out.

"It's the best explanation why you survived so long out here," Gavin replied. "You're immune to the infection."

8

Gavin didn't want to tell her about the experiments, or about the hours he had logged in searching for the cure. He had worked with immune animals of all different species, but Stella was the first immune human he had ever seen.

He had known that Stella was immune from the first moment he saw her and was surprised when he realized the others had no idea what she was. Gavin had even questioned himself, after seeing that she was on the oxygen pill. It was, after all, the first time he had ever been out of the factory. Perhaps he was jumping to conclusions, his curious mind seeing more than what was really there.

He had said nothing about it, merely watching her instead. Then he noticed that though she was on the oxygen pill, she never seemed to be keeping track of the hours like anyone else who depended on them. Then she had mentioned that she had a stash of oxygen pills saved up, with no explanation of where they came from. Lastly, Gavin noticed the fact that Stella didn't follow the routines and rules of the rest of her gang. If none of the others in the gang knew that Stella was immune, at least Xander did. He knew that Stella didn't need to follow the same precautions, and he left her to do as she pleased.

Instead of mentioning all of this, Gavin stated a simple truth. "It's the best explanation why you survived so long out here. You're immune to the infection."

Stella looked directly at him, violet eyes still hazy with pain. "Don't tell anyone."

Gavin didn't ask why; he just nodded in agreement.

Stella closed her eyes as Gavin tied off the end of his makeshift bandage. As she leaned her slight weight against his chest, he tried not to let himself get distracted by the warmth of her skin or the soft intake of air as she caught her breath. He wrapped one of his arms against her back, steadying her. Gavin held her for a few long moments before she whispered, "You ready to get out of here?"

They went back to the van, which Gavin had left running in his haste to get at the infected that had nearly bit its way through Stella's arm. She opened the door wide, letting the corpses fall out and hit the asphalt. Gavin felt the first stirring of exhilaration as Stella changed gear and began to drive down the street. They were getting out of the city, away from this infestation. Gavin supposed that now he could get initiated into their gang, whatever that meant.

The sight of everything blurring past them as the van drove was new and unsettling. He hadn't ever been in a fast-moving machine before, and seeing the rush of motion while he was sitting still was strange.

Stella drove down the clear main street, passing by their Dunkin' Donuts, before abruptly stopping the van and jumping out without a word.

Gavin pressed against the window as Stella ran into a tourist shop. He hesitated, holding on to the car door, trying to see whether she needed his help. Before he could make up his mind, Stella was already running back to the van, wearing a hooded sweatshirt with "I heart New York" emblazoned in neon colors. She stepped back into the van, holding out a shirt and hat bearing the same logos for Gavin, along with a pair of plain jeans.

"Here, put this on," Stella instructed as Gavin picked up the clothes awkwardly. "When we get back, you need to blend in." Stella changed gears and got the van moving again. "Just take out the things you need from the factory and find a place to keep them safe."

Gavin began to pull his tools out of the pockets: vials, syringes, forceps, oxygen pills, and other small machines. For lack of a better place to put them, he started to line up his things in the cup holder of the van. It wasn't until his pockets were empty that Gavin began to feel uncomfortable.

"There's nowhere to get changed," Gavin stated as the van was driving onto a ramp that led back to the George Washington Bridge.

"Don't worry, I won't look." Stella kept her eyes on the road. She waited about ten seconds before glancing at the mortified expression on Gavin's face and grinning. "I was just kidding. I'll stop somewhere and get out when we're away from New York."

Just as Gavin found his emotions settling down, a flash of movement in the street caught his attention. A young infected with stringy hair and greasy, thin limbs was walking toward the van. Stella's eyes were on the infected, and she didn't make any move at all to change her hands on the steering wheel. The crunch of metal reverberated throughout the van, followed by a tilting sensation as the passenger side tires lifted over a bump, one after the other.

Gavin braced his arms, holding himself in place against

the jerking motion, until the tires hit flat pavement once more. He looked in the rear window to see the infected lying motionless in the road behind them. Stella had dispatched the creature without saying a word.

How many times had she had to kill the infected before it became a common part of her life? How long had it taken before she didn't even need to mention the deaths at all? How many of those kills had been close calls, like it had been today, back in the city? Gavin thought back to the fact that she was immune. She had to put herself at risk every day out here, but her life didn't have to be that way.

Gavin struggled against his curiosity until he couldn't hold it in any longer. He had to ask her. "Why haven't you told anyone?"

"It's not safe." An amused grin, left over from teasing him, slipped away from her face. She focused on the clear roads ahead.

Gavin was still trying to think of a way to ask her another question when Stella spoke again. "There's a group of men underground that run the city called the administrators. Many of them are old, older than the rest of the survivors, and in different stages of infection." As Stella spoke, her hands tightened on the steering wheel. "They organized construction underground, but they built in doors with locks, too. To keep out the infected, they said. That's what gave them control, what lets them decide who can get food and pills and who can die. Some of them are half-crazed with infection, with bodies holding together, but their minds starting to go. They'll do anything for a cure."

Gavin listened to the soft sounds of her breathing, which came in short, little gasps of air. It was the only sound of her agitation, the sign that showed him how much the conversation bothered her.

"You think they would hurt you if they knew?" he asked.

There was a pause, as if Stella was trying to decide whether she wanted to tell him. She was quiet for long enough that Gavin worried that he had pushed the conversation too far.

"My father didn't just die. He was murdered," Stella said, breaking the silence. Her voice was tense, as if she had to force each word out.

"I saw it," Stella added so quietly that Gavin could barely hear her. She leaned in closer to the steering wheel and stared blankly at the road. Her eyes glazed over as she thought of things that were far away, reliving memories. "I saw it and I couldn't..." Stella's voice broke, and she had to take a deep, steadying breath. She forced herself to continue. "There were too many. They just killed him, and it happened so fast. I wasn't there to save him, or even help him. I watched it all through the window. Even took his body away, so there was nothing left."

A tear trickled down her cheek, and without thinking about it, Gavin reached over and brushed it away. She reached her hand to her cheek and wrapped it over his, interlacing their fingers. Neither of them said another word as Stella drove them across the George Washington Bridge and away from New York City. She didn't let go of Gavin's hand.

THEY MUST HAVE BEEN QUITE THE SIGHT, DRIVING BACK TO THE base with a van stocked with supplies and wearing New York memorabilia. Stella drove the van straight to the entrance before braking abruptly, right in front of a group assembled outside. There was Xander, Sam, and five other gang members whom Gavin hadn't yet had a chance to meet. All of them carried weapons: machetes, crowbars, and bats, along with the firearms holstered at their sides. They broke off their meeting and turned to stare at Stella and Gavin through the windshield.

Stella ducked her head low as she turned off the ignition. Without looking in Gavin's direction, she whispered, "There's something going on. Stick close." She opened the vehicle door and stepped out.

Walking to the side of the van, Stella wrenched the doors open and exposed the boxes stacked within. She had wasted no time in showing off their haul. As Gavin stepped out to help her, he realized that even the shirts from New York were part of the show, proof that they had done what they had set out to do. Xander approached the van, a grim look on his face.

Ignoring the cans, Xander pulled Stella close to him and hugged her. Gavin stiffened, completely thrown off. He froze, unsure of what to do with himself.

Xander whispered, "I was worried about you."

Stella laughed, slipping out of his grasp. "I told you I'd be all right."

She turned her back to Xander, taking hold of one of the boxes without looking at him.

Xander signaled for the rest of the group to help before grabbing a box and heading after Stella. Gavin lifted a box and trailed after them, watching the pair closely.

"How has the city changed since you were a kid?" Xander stepped closer to Stella until they were side by side.

"It's worse. Completely infested. The food'll dry out in a couple of years like everything else out here," Stella replied.

"Did you get into any trouble?" Xander asked, watching her.

"Nothing that we couldn't handle," Stella said, and Gavin noticed the faint trace of a scowl on Xander's face when she said "we" instead of "I."

Gavin shifted the box in his hands nervously, wondering if he should slow down and put some space between them. But Xander continued to ignore him, and Gavin's curiosity drove him on.

"Anything happen while we were away?" Stella turned the corner and started down a hallway ending in heavy double doors.

"Sam reported a problem with Celia's gang, and we're following up on that now," Xander said.

"What sort of a problem?" Stella was calm.

So Sam followed up on her advice to check out the other gang. But any thoughts Stella had about the mention of her friend, she kept hidden.

"Sam was under the impression that the whole gang is dead," Xander replied in a grim tone. His expression didn't change at all—as if he always expected the worst.

Stella's eyes widened as she did a double take.

A whole gang?

If the numbers were comparable to Xander's gang, that had to be at least twenty to thirty members. That many people should be able to hold off the infected. A general lack of supplies wouldn't take out the whole group at once.

What could cause death on that scale?

"Let's find out, then." Stella pushed through the double doors.

WHEN THE BOXES WERE ALL STASHED AWAY, STELLA DROVE them down the sand-covered road. Gavin found himself in the back of the van with several men he didn't know. He tried to make eye contact with Sam, but the other man wasn't looking his way, so he resigned himself to silence.

As Gavin adjusted to the vibration and jostling of driving, he tuned out the conversations of the other men. He found his eyes drifting every so often to Stella and Xander in the front seat, trying to figure out the dynamics of their relationship.

"Gavin," came Sam's voice, breaking him out of his thoughts. "Ben asked you what you do."

Gavin turned to look at the man that Sam indicated as Ben. He had a riot of tight black curls, graying at the edges, and a lined face. "Mechanical work mostly," Gavin answered simply, aware that the conversations around them had ended as the other men listened for his answer.

"So Stella found you," Ben said, though he already knew the answer.

Gavin nodded curtly in reply.

Ben motioned Gavin to come closer, and he scooted over after casting one hasty glance at the front of the van. "Stay away from her," he whispered faintly. Seeing Gavin's frown, Ben explained, "That's the girl Xander wants. If he thinks you're getting between him and his girl, you're dead."

"What does Stella think about him?" Gavin asked quietly before he could stop himself.

Ben hesitated, casting a swift glance at the other men. "Doesn't matter. Women don't make it out of the underground as often as men. Xander would replace you easily. Seen it plenty of times before."

Gavin nodded in understanding. That explained a lot. It was the other men's fear that kept them away from Stella. She was only free to hang around Sam because he was in a relationship with another woman. But just because Xander wanted Stella didn't mean that she returned his feelings.

"We'll be there in five minutes," Stella announced, watching the men in the rearview mirror. Gavin caught Stella's eye in the mirror and held her gaze for a moment before forcing himself to look back down. He didn't know what to do. He had never let himself get this close to anyone else before, and he wasn't sure if he was willing to just let her go.

It wasn't that she was beautiful, or even that she was immune, that drew him to Stella. Gavin saw through her fierce exterior to the kindness beneath it. He knew she easily could have let him die, but she was driven to help him survive. He couldn't think of anyone else like her who would dare to take on even a fraction of the risks Stella faced.

The movement of the van slowed down and the brakes screeched before the van came to a stop.

Celia's gang lived in a building that looked like it was taken straight out of the yellowed textbook pages of fortresses built in the Middle Ages. The grand building was made of high stone towers stained gray with sand and time. The chipped lettering high on the left wall read "Hilton." Even from the outside, an unnatural, oppressive quiet hung over the building.

The other men looked to Sam, who crossed his arms nervously before he began walking toward the building. With the bent metal of a Swiss Army knife, Sam picked at the lock on an emergency exit until, with a soft click, the door swung forward.

Harsh fluorescent lights illuminated the emergency stairwell, and the droning hum of electricity was the only sound to be heard. They followed Sam up the stairs, and Gavin caught more than one man clenching a sharpened weapon, more than one hand straying close to a gun holster.

"They were on the fifth floor," Sam said, breaking the silence. Xander nodded him on, and the group made their way up cautiously.

Gavin heard the reactions before he saw it. The footsteps shuffled and ground to a halt, and the others ahead of him slowed down. The little groan of distaste and the soft whispered curse word probably came from Stella. He had that one extra moment to prepare himself before he followed the rest of them in.

When Gavin walked out of the stairway and into the hall, he only saw two bodies at first, lying still on the ground. An ugly black line marked where the bodies touched the floor as gravity pulled dead blood cells down. If this dependent lividity had already set in, then these men were indeed dead and had been so for a while.

The others were farther ahead, having passed this pair of corpses without a word. Gavin tore his eyes away and continued walking, dreading to see exactly what it would take to get a reaction out of someone like Stella, or any of the others who were accustomed to death.

At first, all Gavin could see was the sleek maple table surrounded by leather chairs. It took a moment for his brain to process the devastation. Then the awareness of what had happened here in this room settled in, the weight of it pooled into the pit of his stomach, and his muscles tightened in anxiety, tense and ready to act.

There were bodies, many of them. It was obvious from their contorted positions and from the painful grimaces still etched on their faces that none of these people had died natural deaths.

"What the hell is this?" someone whispered.

"I've never seen anything like it," another one said.

The worst part was that Gavin knew. It only had taken

him one glance to recognize the symptoms. The tests they had run were still etched in his memory. He knew exactly what had happened to them, and who was responsible. The only question left for him to answer was how.

Xander was the first one to come out of his shocked daze. He turned to Ben, who stopped gawking at the sight and snapped to attention.

"Take a team and do a security sweep. Bring back any survivors and anything that looks out of place," Xander directed.

Ben signaled for four others to follow him, and they strode out of the room. From their tense expressions, some were glad for the excuse to get away from that meeting room.

Xander turned to Sam. "How did you find out about this?" The question was asked in a quiet voice, and it wouldn't have seemed like an out of the ordinary thing to say. Except that Stella looked quickly over at her friend in alarm before turning her head back to survey the room in a forced calm.

Now there was nowhere left for Sam if he got kicked out of Xander's gang, and he had no legitimate reason to have been here. More than anything else, Sam needed time to figure out a new way to keep himself and Natalia safe. He couldn't afford to come under suspicion.

But Sam lied smoothly. "I wasn't having any luck last raid, so I just came near to see if Celia's gang was doing any better. Things were too quiet, and I thought something had to be wrong."

"So you entered into enemy territory alone? On nothing more than a hunch?" Xander asked skeptically.

"I knew something big must have happened. There's no other way a gang as big as Celia's could be that quiet," Sam replied, refusing to acknowledge that he had done anything wrong.

At any rate, Xander didn't push the issue. He kneeled close to one of the bodies before turning next to Stella. "Have you ever seen anything like this before?"

Stella looked carefully at the bodies on the floor. "No, never. What about you, Gavin? Have you seen this before?"

Gavin didn't know what to say. He just nodded his head yes. Stella faltered when she saw his nod, and Gavin wondered if he had made a mistake.

Everyone in the room—Stella, Sam, and Xander—were all staring at him. He felt the weight of those stares. He no longer had the option to sit tight and keep the truth all to himself.

"They died because they took defective oxygen pills," Gavin said quietly. When no one responded to his statement, Gavin realized that he had to explain.

"When the oxygen is harvested, the pills need to be able to withstand a lot of pressure. The pills have to be able to hold and release the right amount of gases to exchange in the lungs over time." Gavin walked over to one of the bodies of a girl who had died clutching her chest. "Defective pills can't hold the pressure. They go into the body and work for a while, then all the gas gets released at once. That's why her chest is contorted, from when the pill exploded in her lungs." Gavin lifted her hand out of the way to reveal the misshapen bulge where all the gases tried to escape. He didn't want to mention that all the pus seeping out from her eyes, nostrils, and mouth were the liquefied remains of organs that were forced out of her. It was a horrible way to die.

Gavin noticed that the others were all still quiet. All he

had done was tell the truth. But he wondered if that had been enough.

"You believe this guy?" Xander said, breaking the silence. He had directed the question to Stella.

She straightened from where she had crouched to examine the body and stared Xander directly in the eye. "Yes, I do."

Xander scowled at her show of support. "They don't make defective pills. I've never seen one in my life."

"They are made, but they get tested and they don't get shipped out," Gavin explained.

"If they don't get shipped, then what are they doing here?" Xander asked again.

"I don't know." Gavin had been wondering the same thing. He couldn't rid himself of the suspicion that things going wrong here meant that not everything was safe back at his home, either.

Xander had opened his mouth to ask another question when they were interrupted by the return of Ben and his team. Ben hesitated for a moment when he saw how close Xander and Gavin were standing and saw the irritated expression on Xander's face. Ben didn't say anything until Xander stepped away and turned his attention back to him.

"No survivors," Ben reported. "We found more bodies scattered around, but nothing out of the ordinary. Only strange thing is they got themselves a whole shipment of oxygen pills. And Celia's gang doesn't go underground for raids." Ben handed over a sample of the green pills to Xander.

"So I suppose you're going to tell me that all those pills are defective," Xander said, rounding on Gavin once more. Gavin took a look at the pills and saw that they were unmarked, unlike those that had been tested and approved for shipment. He replied once more with just a nod, not sure of what to say around Xander.

Xander shoved the pills aggressively close to Gavin's face. "Prove it."

Gavin picked up a pill, dropped it to the ground, and stomped on it with his boot. The pill erupted with a bang like a gunshot, leaving a crater of cracked marble. The little green pill spun in a circle, hissing as all the gas leaked out of it.

"Good pills don't do that," Gavin replied calmly.

"I'd say that you just destroyed a perfectly good pill," Xander disagreed. "Why should we waste a whole shipment of perfectly good pills on your word? You're just going to have to find another way to prove your little theory."

Gavin sighed in frustration. He wasn't used to having to explain his every action and justify the things he knew. Back home, all of this was common knowledge. But he couldn't risk that they'd take the pills—they were lethal.

He looked once at Stella and saw the worry in her eyes that she tried to hide. He didn't want her to have to feel like she had to look out for him all the time. He was just going to have to reveal a little of what he could do.

Gavin reached into an inner pocket where he had hidden the machine. He ran his finger across the cool metal, switching it on. It unraveled out of its tight coil, spreading out its mechanical wings. The lights on the machine's little face flickered on as it hummed to life. The wings began flapping up and down with a mechanical whirring noise, faster and faster until it became a blur. Then the machine, which now resembled a little mechanical hummingbird, jerked into the air and swooped around in quick, circular patterns. Then it really began to fly, zooming its sporadic path over and around everyone in the room, avoiding obstacles with agile grace.

The others watched, completely transfixed. All eyes remained set on the little metal bird. After a minute, the machine flew back toward Gavin, who reached out for it. The bird landed in the palm of his hand, nestling down as if it had returned to a home made of sticks and twigs. The lights dimmed from its eyes and the machine curled up once again into a tight ball. When Gavin removed it from his hand, they could all see that it had deposited one green pill there. An oxygen pill.

Gavin placed the machine back into his inner pocket. "I know those pills you have found are defective because I help harvest oxygen back at the factory."

The understanding lit up in the faces around the room. The men who had regarded him before with indifference now stared at him openly, shocked.

Xander approached Gavin differently, with that same caution he had briefly shown when they had first met. He picked up the oxygen pill out of Gavin's hand for a closer examination, rolling it around between his thumb and index finger.

"You're not going to want to take that," Gavin warned him. "That one will be contaminated with traces of the open air. It's no good."

"You said that you worked as a mechanic," Xander replied, still focused on the oxygen pill like he had never seen one before.

"That's most of what I do, building the machines. But there's a lot of other work there." Gavin thought through his lists of odd jobs. "Plants and animals to raise, tests to run. Sometimes I help my brother with the collection and distribution of resources."

"Can I see that bird thing of yours?" Xander asked.

Gavin paused before he reached back into his pocket, taking out the machine once again. "It's keyed into my fingerprints, so it will only work for me," he said as Xander fiddled with the machine, trying to figure out how to activate it. "It's useless here anyway, out in open air."

"You built this." Xander held the machine up close to his pale eyes.

"I did," Gavin answered, wondering where the conversation was headed.

"So you know how to build other machines? Could you help us to make our own oxygen pills here?" Xander's eyes narrowed in cold calculation.

Gavin thought about everything that Xander was asking for, the tools and materials for the job and the sheer scope of the task. Yes, it would take time, but it was possible.

"I'll help you make your own oxygen pills if you change one of your rules," Gavin offered, struck suddenly with an idea.

"I don't negotiate the rules," Xander said. "And you might want to rethink bargaining with me. This isn't your factory. Things could get pretty dangerous out here for you." Xander rested his hand casually against his side so it was just touching his gun holster.

Around the room, the others reacted to the threat, some even moving slightly in Gavin's defense before stopping themselves.

"There are three people in the world who know how to build that machine," Gavin said, unperturbed. "And the other two are back in a factory under the ocean. Killing me won't get you anything."

"What rule do you want changed?" Xander asked.

"The rule against pregnancy. The one that says that your gang members can't have babies," Gavin said.

Xander blinked in surprise. Distracted, he glanced over at Stella. "Why that rule?"

"If there's no kids, there's no future here. No point in building anything if it'll just be useless in a hundred years when there's no one left," Gavin replied.

Xander rolled the machine between his thumb and pointer finger.

"Fine," Xander said at last. "You've got yourself a deal."

9

Stella wanted to smash that mechanized hummingbird into pieces. She had seen Xander tracking the movements of that little bird. She knew that calculating look. Even after taking Gavin into an infested city to avoid suspicion, his cover was blown. She knew what Xander would want to do with a scientist from the *factory*.

Stella watched Gavin in the rearview mirror as she began the drive back. He looked merely uncomfortable with all the stares. He had no idea about the kind of trouble he had brought down upon himself. With all the increased attention on him, Gavin was never going to be able to just slip away. All eyes were going to be on him from here on out.

Stella drove in quiet anger, and she wasn't alone in her silence. The men in the back of the van watched Gavin in open curiosity. It was only a matter of time before one of them gathered up the courage to ask him about the factory.

Though it wasn't something that anyone talked about, everyone knew about the oxygen factory. Everyone knew that it existed. The proof came in the weekly shipments that arrived every Monday without fail. Little was known about the factory. Not about how it started, or how it operated. Anyone who said differently was probably lying. All of humankind depended on the shipments from the factory. Everyone would be dead within weeks without it.

"Is it true what they say about the oxygen factory?" Dan blurted out, breaking the silence. No longer able to resist the temptation, when all this forbidden knowledge sat right across from him.

"What do they say about it?" Gavin picked his head up to look at Dan.

"That it's filled with hundreds of animals. That they do all sorts of experiments. That they have a cure for the infection. That the people who live there never get sick, and that no one that lives there has ever died," Dan said all in a rush.

All of their heads seemed to lean toward Gavin, waiting for his answer. Even Xander in the front seat quit his silent reflections to listen in.

"No," Gavin replied mildly. "That's not true. Except for the part about the experiments. We do those."

"How did you get there?" Sam cut in.

"I was brought to the factory when I was a baby. I don't remember anything before." Gavin loosened his arms from their tight grip across his chest as he spoke about his home.

"Where is it?" Sam asked again.

"The factory is under the ocean, along the Atlantic coast. Approximately fifty or sixty miles away from here." Gavin gestured in the direction of the shore, as if he could just touch it.

Sam paused, seeming startled by the specificity of the answer. "Could we get there from here?"

"You could try, but you might get eaten along the way. The toxins had a bad effect on some of the aquatic life." Gavin shook his head.

"What kind of foods do they have at the oxygen factory?" Ben called out.

In spite of her anger, Stella found herself fighting against a grin. Out of all the questions he could have asked, Ben was mainly interested in the food.

"The same things that we ship out to everyone else," Gavin said simply.

"But you said you don't eat meat. Is that a rule or something there?" Sam asked.

"No, that's just me. I couldn't eat meat anymore after I started helping out with slaughtering the pigs." Gavin shut his eyes briefly as if shutting out a bad memory.

"How many pigs did you have to kill?" Dan asked.

"I've done thousands. After I became a vegetarian, though, I got taken off that shift permanently. I think my father was worried I wouldn't be a good worker anymore without the protein or something."

His easy answers loosened up the tongues of the others.

"If there aren't hundreds of animals at the factory, how many are there?"

"There are half a million different animal species. Many are living specimens and others are blood samples awaiting regeneration," Gavin said.

"How big is the factory?" Dan asked.

"About the size of a small city, but it expands every year," Gavin explained. "It's organized into four different harvest domes. We live in the center where the domes meet."

"How did they build the factory under the ocean?"

"No, who built it?"

Gavin was cut off from answering as something in the engine popped with a blast like a gunshot. The van jolted and lurched forward. Stella heard the thud as the men in the back were jostled into one another.

The steering wheel reverberated under her hands and Stella braced her weight against it, fighting to keep the van driving straight. The engine rolled to a halt, sputtering angrily as it died out.

After turning the ignition once more and hearing a loud, screeching whine, she gave up and turned off the engine.

When Stella stepped outside, Gavin was already in the front of the van, prying open the hood.

"Get back, we have to move out," Xander ordered. When he saw Gavin hesitate by the engine, he continued, "A hundred infected just heard that. I don't care what you can do, it's not worth the risk."

The men, who had been so busy with questions just moments before, fell silent. None of them would speak up to suggest that they try things a new way. Their old fears and reliance on Xander's rules settled everything back into place.

For Xander, safety wasn't a goal; it was a compulsion. It went back as far as Stella could remember, when Xander was twelve and she was eight. Those days he would check his watch many hundreds of times a day. He would start warning Stella and her dad of the time even three hours before the infected were likely to come out.

Xander had adopted the guidelines that Stella and her father had lived by and turned them into the Rules:

Be armed.

Travel in a group or in pairs.

Remain quiet.

Know where the exits are.

Avoid the infected.

Avoid contact with potential infected.

Over short distances, kill the infected silently.

Only fire at the infected over long distances.

Do NOT engage in noisemaking, including, but not limited to, screams, power tools, and childbirth.

Do NOT endanger the living for the dead or the potential dead.

Do NOT go out into the night.

At least, those were the rules that Stella had bothered to remember. Over the years at the gang, she began to see new rules trickle in, rules and laws and procedures that were starting to blur the lines between the freedoms they had and the lives of those who lived underground. The punishments for breaking the rules were starting to outweigh any gains they had made in safety.

Stella knew exactly how Xander would see Gavin now. Gavin was more than just a new rule. Gavin was more than a project or method that could make their lives easier. Gavin was someone who had lived completely outside of all of their systems and outside of everything they knew—a glimpse of a safe world. She had delivered Gavin straight into Xander's hands, without even giving him any kind of warning.

Stella caught Gavin's eye and shook her head discreetly, telling him no. Now was not the time. She had no doubts that Gavin could fix the van, just as she knew that Xander would never agree to it.

Besides, it was getting late.

She looked across the landscape, the sand once again taking on a reddish hue with the sun low on the dunes. In less than two hours, the infected would begin to wake. Or just those they hadn't already awoken from their automobile trouble.

Stella stepped over to Gavin's side. She ignored Xander's gaze following her, just as she ignored his one raised eyebrow. She might as well have built a New York billboard in flashing lights that said she liked Gavin. Right now, she couldn't care about that.

"They're coming," Stella murmured, in a voice low enough that only he would hear it. "Step away from the van and stick close."

Stella walked away from the van, distancing herself from the others out in the open. After a beat, Gavin joined her.

"This is just the quiet that comes before," Stella whispered. "They know we're here."

One building had caught her attention. It was too open, with cracked windows and a discarded door ripped straight off its hinges. Stella quickly noted all the signs of the infected, from the size of the building to the droppings, right down to the claw marks cutting into the wood. It was exactly the sort of building she had learned to avoid.

Inside, Stella could start to see shapes moving in the shadows, just little subtle shifts where the darkness became darker. There was no question in her mind that they were there. The only question that mattered was how many.

She was already unconsciously reaching for her gun. Their group was too large to just slip away. They would have to act fast. They were running out of time to fight.

Stella aimed her Glock, alerting the others. Without looking, she could sense her gang falling into position around her. Her attention was trained on that dark space between four corners of an open door. Right now, that was the only space that mattered.

Ragged, blackened fingernails curved around the door-frame. The nails dug into wood as an infected pulled itself into view. A dirt-streaked face emerged out of the gloom with nostrils flaring wide.

A shot fired out, and the hand fell out of view.

Stella gritted her teeth just as she heard Xander murmur, "Damn it."

THAT GUNSHOT WAS TOO EARLY. IF THEY HAD WAITED, MORE infected would file out of the building. Then they could take down as many as possible and bolt.

It couldn't be helped. New gang members rarely developed that cold patience needed to survive out here. Most of them had only been out from underground for a year or two. Many of them would only last a year or two longer.

The infected could sense when one of their fellows was taken down, especially this close to their home. That shot could awaken their hive mind.

Stella doubled the grip on her Glock and braced herself. She counted down the time in her mind, all the while watching how the movement behind the door went terribly still.

The infected erupted out in a swarm. Their swaying, outstretched arms blurred together into one. Watching all of those cracked teeth and wretched bodies was dizzying. Stella forced herself to tune in to individual features and just pick one out of the many. She locked onto a pair of sunken eyes and fired.

Stella watched it fall to the ground with a shot through the forehead. Those directly behind it stumbled to the ground. It only briefly slowed them down. The fallen infected pushed themselves to their feet, scrambling over the others still on the ground. All too soon they were upright and rushing forward in a blind run, with arms extended and mouths gaping.

Stella fired again and again, counting the shots around

her. They were only outnumbered two to one, but it was enough. They were so close.

Screams cut off Stella's mental count. Her eyes flicked over to Gavin, who was unharmed, before finding the source of the sound. Two of them had gotten to Dan.

Stella could already tell that it was too late. She blasted a hole through the head of one that had sunk its claws into Dan's arm, just as the second one leaned forward and bit straight into his neck.

Dan's eyes clenched shut—he knew what it meant. As the infected latched on tighter, a wail slipped out of his lips, louder than before. Stella knew from experience that he wouldn't have expected the power behind the bite, which forced those jagged teeth to saw their way into his flesh.

Dan's scream distracted the infected. They froze in inde- cision, torn between the need to protect their home and the drive to feed. Stella took the opportunity. She targeted the infected closest to him and took them out. She dashed toward Dan, ignoring Xander's yell. "Stella!"

She maneuvered just close enough and got one clean shot.

She watched the infected's head jerk back and dislodge from its grip on Dan. She watched in satisfaction as it dropped to the ground. She had to stop herself from firing once more in revenge. Instead, Stella looked up and assessed her surroundings, just in time to see the last of the infected around her taken down.

Stella didn't even have enough time to tell Dan to get up and move before Xander reached them, gun drawn and pointed straight at Dan's forehead.

"He has two days," Stella argued. "Maybe a few more if he's lucky."

"It's going to happen anyway. He's just going to put us at

risk," Xander stated.

Stella replied softly, barely moving her lips so that the others wouldn't know what was said. "That's something an administrator would do. You're better than that." Xander paused, considering, and Stella added, "Give him a chance to say goodbye. We can always shoot him later."

Xander directed his attention back to Dan. "We've gotta move, and we aren't slowing down for you. Keep up or get left behind."

"Fine. Just don't kill me," Dan managed to get out, clutching his bite wound without looking at either of them.

"Night falls in an hour and forty minutes. Move," Xander commanded the rest of them.

They didn't need any coaxing. The noise from the shots would wake more infected, alerting them to this location. It was just a matter of time before this place was swarming with them. Weapons in hand, they took off in the direction of their base, passing the infected that were just waking and cocking heads in their direction as they listened after them.

As they returned to their base, a pale-faced Dan was pushed inside. The bottom of his shirt was ripped off and pressed against his wounds. Stella swallowed at the sight of it. The makeshift bandages were soaked, but not leaving a trail.

Dan would spend the rest of his days in the same containment room she'd recently gotten Gavin out of—a room few people walked out of alive.

How much of her blood would it take to save him? Stella never saw the people who got their hands on her blood. Dan wasn't just exposed to toxins. He was *bitten*. His body was overloaded with infection. Trying to save him would probably kill her.

As Stella tried to follow the others inside, Xander

demanded to speak with her. He wasn't subtle about it either. He just grabbed her wrist, halting her. It wasn't like him to linger outside at any time. Especially this close to dark.

Stella did not even spare Gavin a glance as she allowed herself to be pulled away. It wouldn't help things. Whatever else he was, Gavin was safe for now.

As soon as they were alone, Xander said, "You knew about Gavin."

Stella nodded in reply.

"What do you want from him?" he asked.

"I want what everyone else wants. I want to survive. Right now, keeping Gavin alive is what we need to do to survive."

"No. There's more to it than that." Xander stepped closer to her.

"Of course there is. He's from the oxygen factory. We've never met anyone like him before. Would you expect me to treat him the same as everyone else?"

"Yes. I guess that makes sense." Xander grabbed the bridge of his nose in frustration. "But you could have told me. Avoided all of this."

Stella looked away. Once, perhaps, she would have gone straight to him. But he was different then.

She didn't know what he planned for Gavin. But whatever it was, Gavin deserved better than to be used. She needed to get him home.

"We were out late today," Stella said, changing the topic.

"We had a last-minute change of plans." Xander ripped his gaze away from Stella.

"That's not like you." Stella frowned. Xander's usual style was to plan things like this days in advance, down to the last detail. Xander was efficiency incarnate.

"There was something that I had to do. Something that was more than just survival." Xander averted his eyes.

It wasn't like him to be vague.

"And that had something to do with Celia's gang?" Stella asked. The more she thought about it, the less it made sense. When she had gotten back to base, Xander was standing outside, armed and just about to head out. Come to think of it, Xander didn't usually go out with those kinds of numbers just to check up on a rival gang. No. He had planned to go out somewhere that he knew was going to be dangerous.

Xander just shook his head no. Stella wondered if he was going to keep silent when he replied, "I couldn't stop worrying. I was wrong to let you go out there in the first place."

He took Stella's wrist carefully in his hands and began pulling away her sleeves until he uncovered her injury. Xander stared at that dark red, seeping through the layers of gauze. "You got bit again." He must have been quietly watching her to have noticed the subtle difference between her two sleeves.

It suddenly clicked together. Stella was so surprised that she said it out loud. "I was that change. You were going to go into the city after me."

"I couldn't think of anything else for the past two days, just that you could be killed and it would be all my fault," Xander said, running his hands through his hair like he did when he was really annoyed at himself. "I'm sorry."

Xander had planned to run into the city after her. He had been about to break almost every one of his rules for her. And for the first time, Xander was apologizing. Stella really didn't know what to say.

10

As Xander strode to the conference room, he noticed Paul, a new recruit, steer straight out of his way and back up flat against the wall. Xander could easily see the whites of Paul's wide eyes. With each step closer, Paul scrunched his limbs tighter against his body, as if he wanted nothing more than to press into the wall and disappear.

Xander stopped, watching Paul's slight frame tense up.

Xander could have ignored Paul and kept walking. He had plenty of other things to do and a long day of paperwork waiting for him. Instead, he heard Stella's words from last night echoing in his ears. *That's something an administrator would do. You're better than that.* Paul wasn't the only new recruit to see him as an administrator. Some of the older gang members had the same reaction. Not that he was surprised. Xander had been halfway down the road to becoming one before he was forced out of the underground.

"Paul," Xander said, watching him flinch. "This isn't the underground, and that isn't necessary."

Paul's only response was to cast his gaze down to the floor.

"What was your section?" Xander asked him.

"South, Sir," Paul replied in a small voice. Paul certainly looked the part. The south housed all the menial task workers in food production and maintenance. Yet there had to be more to this skinny recruit if he had somehow managed to escape all the way from the south. More still, seeing as he had survived his initiation.

"Look at me." Xander waited until dark eyes reluctantly met his own. "I don't know who you were in the city, and I don't care. Here, you're my soldier. You don't ever back down, not even from me. You aren't south section anymore."

Paul nodded, keeping his eye contact. It was slight, but Xander noticed a shift in Paul's stance as he straightened. Paul watched in curiosity as Xander continued on his way.

Xander unlocked his conference room. Laid across the mahogany table were diagrams and maps he had carefully constructed from memory. Xander ran his fingers down the largest map, which showed the layout of the entire underground city. His finger traced familiar paths he had used, lingering on potential obstacles. After a moment, his fingers drifted away to the southeastern corner of the map and rested on the faint indent of erasure marks under the administrators' lounge.

He didn't look up when he heard a knock.

"Bring him in," Xander said, just loud enough to be heard.

The door swung open, and there was the heavy thud of boots as the visitor stepped into the room. Xander listened as the footfalls came nearer, stopping right beside him.

"Tell me more about your machines," Xander said, keeping his eyes on the map. Depending on what materials they needed, Xander would have to arrange a raid on the city. It wouldn't be an ordinary raid, either. Normally, a small team could go in every few weeks and take or trade what they needed. A basic supply of pills and food was easy enough to arrange. Underground citizens practically giftwrapped it for them to avoid gang retaliation. With a handful of people and the right strategy, his gang was in and out. In this case, some of the more delicate tools and equipment were in the southwest corridors, located deeper into the city. Getting at those supplies required a more sophisticated strategy. Time to send the underground a reminder of what they were capable of.

"This is the underground city." The scientist, Gavin, peered over the map. "Here, this symbol represents the shipment station." The scientist pointed to the north. He was correct. Not that it mattered.

Xander said nothing, waiting for the answer to his question.

"The shipment station will have a control panel. I could just type in my security codes and the submarine should deliver anything I need from the factory," he told Xander.

The scientist really wasn't from around here.

"How much did Stella tell you about the underground?" Xander asked.

"Not much, just that it's dangerous."

Xander quashed his annoyance and the nagging thought that he was wasting time. After all, he was dealing with a scientist. Science dealt with facts in order to function. Xander wasn't going to make progress in this meeting without explaining how things work. "When the infection first hit, everyone was trying to escape in different ways. Some were better at it than others. Around New York City lived some powerful men. Some were politicians, heads of businesses, and some of them were just rich. Those men escaped the infection by working together on underground construction. When those men built, they made sure to design something into the infrastructure that has kept them in power to this day."

"What was it?" the scientist asked.

"Keys," Xander said. "The city is divided into each section of the compass rose, and it is controlled by seven administrators with seven sets of keys. Originally, they explained to everyone that they needed the keys as a fail-safe. If any of the infected got into the underground, there had to be a way to stop the spread. Obviously, that isn't really how they use them."

"How could a couple of keys control a population of over eighty thousand people?"

"Think of all the things the administrators could keep locked away. Food, water, oxygen pills... people. The citizens keep the administrators happy because if they don't, with one turn of a key, they will starve and count down the minutes until their oxygen pills run out."

"We do population counts. We send out more than enough." The scientist leaned closer and gritted his teeth, as if determination alone could change things. His naivety was ridiculous.

The scientist was useful; even Xander had to admit that. Beyond that, Xander had no idea what Stella saw in him.

"It isn't about quantity, it's about control. The people who live underground don't have anywhere else to go. They know that it's infested outside. They live their whole lives listening to administrators explain that *they* built the city. If those people want to live, it's by *their* rules. When people are given hard choices, one of them almost guaranteed to be a brutal death, you would be surprised by what they agree to do."

"Like what?" the scientist asked in a grim tone, as if he

didn't really want to know. "What really happens down there?"

"One of the first things you'll see when you enter the underground city is a hallway of dialysis patients. Dialysis is mandatory for people that start to turn. Most of the citizens think the procedure is meant to heal them. But those machines don't stop the transformation, they only weaken it. They don't know there is a hallway connecting patients to a prison monitored by the advance guards. You see, those men like to be able to practice their skills."

"They turn people on purpose." The scientist shook his head with a dazed look on his face, as if he couldn't believe it. But Xander wasn't quite done.

"The worst is at the far end of the city, in the east section. The administrator in charge there is a real piece of work. That bastard goes around the city, buying up the contracts of the prettiest women he can find. He likes to call it the 'entertainment' work, and once he's got them, those women can't get out, whether they want to or not. They know all about the prisons—if they don't go along with everything his soldiers desire, that is exactly where they'll end up." Xander watched the color drain out of Gavin's face as his bitter words sank in.

Getting back to business, Xander tapped on the diagram, drawing in the scientist's attention. "You would enter from the west. Your first locked door would be by the nurse's corridor. The second lock would be at the supply room. From there, you have three more locked hallways. Even if you found your way around, the doors are under constant surveillance and the guards would kill you on sight. You aren't going to get to the shipment station."

The scientist frowned, and a crease furrowed between

his eyebrows as he processed the information. "There should be eight."

"What?"

"You said there was one administrator for every point on the compass. There should be eight. What happened to the missing one?"

He was sharper than Xander had initially given him credit for. And bolder, too.

"You're right. There used to be eight." Xander said dismissively. "The administrators will turn on anyone, even colleagues."

It hadn't been a major event, just petty vengeance as the administrators jostled for power. He had gotten home, his fingers on the doorknob, when he heard it. Not curses or screams, only that half-hearted plea. *"No. Don't."* In the crack under the door, he could make out the crumpled bodies of his parents, more dead than alive, and that awful redness that coated everything. Then he ran.

"Why would they do that?" the scientist asked.

"Differences in opinion." It took Xander years to piece together the story of what happened that day. He knew who ordered the attack and why, but there were things he never managed to figure out. He didn't even know what had happened to his sister, Vivienne. Cautious questions and whispers in the right direction never led anywhere.

But now wasn't the time to think about that four-year-old mop of curls that used to follow him around everywhere.

"So I'll ask again. What do you need to build the machine?" Xander said, redirecting the conversation.

"I'll need a large, enclosed space," the scientist said. "It has to have windows."

Xander nodded, signaling the scientist to continue. He already had a room in mind that should do.

"I'm going to need metals—copper, iron, and steel."

"Metal isn't going to be a problem. Plenty of that lying around out here. Anything else?"

"Some basic tools, like a hammer, screwdriver, blowtorch, wires... That kind of thing," Gavin said.

"That should be simple enough. Should be able to find it in storage in the southwest zone, right by the entrance. We'll have you started on this machine by the afternoon." Xander nodded.

"Right. Then all we'll need is some soil and some seeds to plant, and then we'll be all set."

"Seeds?"

"Seeds," the scientist repeated.

"You're kidding." A smirk formed on Xander's face. "Just when I thought you didn't know anything, you start joking around with me."

"Can't get oxygen without plants. Nothing will work without them," the scientist replied, bemused.

Xander picked up a Sharpie and carefully circled the map three times: once for basic supplies, next for tools, and last for the seeds. That last circle was in the southeast, in the administrators' lounge, almost as far away from the entrance as it was possible to be.

"The best of the food goes straight to the administrators and their guards. That includes all of the fruits and most of the vegetables. Some of the gang have only eaten fruit a handful of times. Stella's never even had it once."

"I can't believe that," the scientist said, looking more crestfallen than he had when he learned about some of the city's worst atrocities. "All that time harvesting, I just assumed that it was actually feeding everyone."

"Getting the seeds isn't going to be easy. We'll need to distract them. We'll go in more numbers than they can handle and to different zones. Should be enough to let a few people slip by unnoticed to get fruit." Xander carefully marked out three routes.

"Are you planning on taking her?"

Xander stiffened. "That's none of your concern."

"You said it yourself that this raid is going to be dangerous." The scientist eyed the map, tracing that long winding path to the seeds.

"Stella is a member of this group. She does her part to keep it going." Xander's hands tightened on the edge of the desk until his knuckles turned white.

"It's riskier for her," the scientist interjected, not knowing when to keep his mouth shut.

"What, you think she's some helpless girl after she saved your ass in New York?" Xander just stopped himself from rolling his eyes.

"I know she's not a helpless girl. She's not weak, but—"

"But what? Please tell me what you have learned in the last two days that makes you an expert on what's best for her." Xander kept his grip locked on his desk, because if he let go, he was going to punch that concerned expression right off the scientist's face. He couldn't do that if he wanted this project to run smoothly.

"But she could be targeted. If the administrators went after her father, it's just a matter of time until they go after her for the exact same reason."

"You act like she doesn't already know that." Xander's heart was beating so fast that he heard the heavy pounding in his ears. Every muscle in his body was wired. More than anything, the fact that the scientist was needed ate away at him as he forced himself not to act. "You might think you know her, but you don't."

Xander stared the scientist down, daring him to say anything. After a moment, he called out to Ben. "Take him to the pool room. Make sure he gets whatever he needs."

Ben entered and stood at the scientist's side to escort him away.

Gavin flashed him a cold, clinical look. As if that look could open Xander up like a machine and see exactly what was inside.

Xander gritted his teeth, looking over his plans as Gavin left.

He would like nothing better than to get out of his chair and slam it against the smooth mahogany—a relic that survived the end of civilization, but could splinter apart under his hands. Xander traced through the map routes instead.

He couldn't get her out of his mind.

For those two days without her, Xander hadn't been able to think. He had been sick with worry. Unbidden thoughts came to his mind of Stella running from the infected, Stella surrounded, Stella motionless and cold, never to come back to him. The thought that there was a threat to her, so close, was intolerable. It was time for him to do something about it.

Xander arranged his plans in a precise order. He gave them a quick look over and, satisfied that they were complete, set them down. He rose from his desk and stretched.

It was a quick walk down a few flights of stairs. He was down in the basement, where the air was cool and moisture clung to the skin. There was no sound here, save for the droning of water pipes.

At the far end, there was a guard posted who hadn't noticed his entrance. The guard was clenching his rifle, completely tuned in to the sounds coming through the containment room.

"Get Ben," Xander ordered. Once dismissed, the guard sprung back, as if the door itself was capable of rearing up and attacking.

One brief image of Stella flitted through his mind, of that first time he had seen her bit and all the quiet horror etched on to her sweet features.

He let himself in.

"Who's there?" Dan called out, startled. He shifted his head from the left to the right, trying to see with clouded eyes. Xander had heard it described as searching for holes in the fog. Black veins marked Dan's arms and shoulders, snaking all the way up to his neck.

As Dan reached one arm out tentatively, he exposed skin that appeared dried out and stretched thin. Even his finger-nails were darkened and chipped into points. He didn't even look human anymore.

"No. Please, no." Dan withdrew instantly and tried to shield himself with his arms as he caught sight of Xander. Dan backed away and pushed himself as far into the containment room as he could.

Xander didn't say a word. He pulled out his Thompson 1911C and shot him.

When Ben arrived, Xander was still wiping down the tar-like blood before it contaminated everything.

Xander threw soiled towels into a trash bag, then stripped off rubber gloves and threw them in as well. "Dump him a mile out. When you come back, I need you to mention this to Sam at the afternoon shift. Tell him that Dan got worse. He couldn't take it anymore."

11

T he sun was obscured by a haze of clouds when Stella found herself once again outside of the entrance to the underground city. All eyes were on Xander as he paused before giving out orders. Stella knew he was running through the corridors in his mind, visualizing every hall, every turn, step by step. They waited until Xander dropped to his knees in front of the entrance that jutted out of the desert floor, metal surrounded by sand.

Xander jammed his weight against the latch, which screeched to an open. They stood around the opening to the underground, staring into the darkness.

"First group, take the hallway through the nurse's zone," Xander ordered.

One by one, the men filed down the spiraling metal staircase. Stella heard boots against metal and watched the backs of their heads circling down until they made their way into the first passageway and she could no longer see them.

It wasn't long before they heard the faint sounds of screaming and the distance pop of gunfire.

"Second group, head to the supply room, and don't hold anything back. Today, we hit them hard," Xander said.

The second group wasn't just the more experienced men. No. Xander had grouped together every gang member with a serious grudge against the city.

Xander turned to Stella. "You ready?" he asked her.

"Just like old times," Stella muttered.

"Not exactly." Xander shook his head. "To get to the fruit, we're going to have to go to the administrators' lounge."

Stella didn't know what to say. She just listened to her heart pounding in her chest, her palm slick with sweat. There was no way. What the hell was Xander thinking, asking the two of them to take a little stroll into the administrators' lounge? He was going to get them killed.

She was frozen. Did Xander expect her to walk right into the lair of men who were only alive because they had feasted on the blood of her father?

"I understand if you don't want to go. I'll go in alone." There was no trace of disappointment in Xander's voice. He meant every word. He wouldn't ask her to do anything that she didn't feel like she could do.

"No," Stella whispered. "No," she said again, forcing her voice to be heard. "I can do this. I'll go. It's just that..." She stopped, leaving the words hanging. She clenched her hands into fists to stop her fingers from shaking. Saying it out loud made it too real. The words were a quiet confession of the power the administrators still held over her.

"I won't let them hurt you," Xander promised. It was true. Xander's desire to protect her was a constant in her life. Obsessed with safety, Xander would look out for her.

He always had.

How could she consider letting him face the administrators alone? He'd have his own demons to face.

Stella patted the familiar weight of the Glock at her side before she grasped the cold metal of the banister. She descended into the underground, following the sounds of chaos below.

Fluorescent lights flickered above with a static, nervous energy. Stella walked at a brisk, straight path, ignoring the citizens who zigzagged in front of her, running in panic. She walked with one hand resting by her hip. Long familiarity made her gun almost an extension of herself.

Xander walked next to her with his pistol out, his hand on the trigger. Alone, Stella would have lurked in the shadows. Now, standing next to Xander, the gang leader and administrator heir, all eyes focused on her—at least until they turned and fled.

Stella heard the sound of marching footsteps, and she casually leaned out of view just as a group of the advance guards ran down a perpendicular corridor.

The usually packed hallways were emptying out from the raids.

This far into the underground, the tunnels were widened and painted crisp white. The recessed light mimicked the brightness of the outdoors. It was too bright. Stella swallowed. The sense of exposure itched at her as anxiety hardened into a pit within her stomach. Stella found her path clear and she continued straight, stepping around a dead body.

All paths in the underground led to the supply room, the lifeline that connected the citizens to basic supplies that arrived in neat packages at the shipping station, straight from the oxygen factory.

All the paths to the supply room also came with their own set of locks, controlled by administrators and their guards. They had to move before the administrators made use of those keys.

They reached the cylinder deadbolt that restricted civilian access to basic essentials. The door was already ajar. Ben had been left out to guard the door to the supply room. He lowered his weapon, and opened the door for them. As they passed, his attention fixed back on securing the entranceway.

The supply room was a tunnel widened to three times the standard size, though it didn't feel larger in the organized chaos of the raid.

A group of maintenance workers lay whimpering in the back corner, terror clear on their faces, with their hands on their heads. The collapsed bodies of the guards were scattered about the room. The first group tore open packages and emptied oxygen pills, bread, and meat into their own bags. One pair was already loaded up, and they took off back into the tunnels.

The supply room was ringed all around with locked doorways, leading to every corner of the underground.

The second group stood in a ring, reloading weapons. One of the new recruits sat on a supply box, putting pressure on a shoulder wound, red seeping through the makeshift bandage.

Pausing briefly to glance at the progress of the raid, Xander walked to one of the doorways that looked older than the others, with chipped paint and an outline where a placard was removed.

He pulled from his pocket a tarnished brass key and unlocked the door. Bracing his back against the frame of the entranceway, Xander pulled the door ajar and listened into the darkness exposed just beyond the supply room.

After a moment of silence, he opened the door fully and

stepped out of the way when a dried-out body slipped from its long rest against wood and fell to the floor. Xander looked closely at the body, which was too small to belong to an adult.

The expression on his face remained the same, and he didn't say a word. Yet he picked the body off of the floor, cradling the bones that wore a faded dress of lilac, with curly wisps of blonde hair still clinging to the small skull.

Xander laid the body down carefully on the floor, just inside the unlocked hallway. He stood near the body, looking away from it, pressing two fingers to his temple.

Stella angled herself in the doorway, blocking Xander from the view of the others, giving him a moment of privacy. Not that the others in the gang didn't have enough on their hands with a raid going on, but he didn't need any wandering eyes or unasked questions. Stella wondered if she should say anything. The girl hadn't been found by the infected outside, or by any of the unsavory individuals here. They could always come back this way and take the little body with them for a proper burial. But she knew Xander too well. It was too much of a risk to jeopardize their lives to take care of the dead. She knew exactly what he would say. It wouldn't change anything.

After a moment, he was himself again.

"Second group, this door leads straight to the administrators' lounge. It hasn't been used in seven years. They won't be expecting it." He paused, waiting out the snickers of his men. "The advance guards will cover the administrators' retreat. Choose your targets well. You won't get another chance."

Xander signaled her over with a glance and Stella stepped farther into the hallway, joining his side. "Stick close," Xander murmured.

They walked in the darkness, the only light being what seeped out from under the door behind them. Not that Stella minded. She was used to the darkness and trained in it. The light could get you overconfident, her father used to say to her. You had to learn to trust the other senses and not just believe in what you could see.

Her senses told her that at least here she was safe. They were the only living things. The first to trod down this path since Xander escaped down this very passageway all those years ago. It wasn't until she began to hear the sounds at the end of the passageway that Stella froze.

She could hear up ahead the clatter of silverware on plates and laughter that was too loud. From up just ahead, Stella could see a new light escaping out from beneath a doorway where the passageway ended. Where *they* were.

She could hear them sitting there, eating, while the underground city fell apart in the raids.

Stella and Xander stood and listened outside the door for a moment, until they both drew out their guns. Stella's Glock and Xander's Thompson 1911C. Silently, Xander unlocked their way in, listening, his hand poised on the doorknob. When he was sure they still had the element of surprise, he kicked the door open.

They opened fire. Stella aimed straight between the eyes of the east section administrator. Her shot hit the guard that dove to protect his boss, and he collapsed to the ground.

Cries rang out as one enormous body slammed to the ground, a bullet hole in the direct center of his forehead. Stella couldn't make out which administrator Xander took down, before the guards swarmed the body, carting it away.

The guards in the room ran to cover the retreat of administrators, and it was their bodies that fell to the ground, over and over.

The administrators ducked low, abandoning their food as they all scattered away, running in all directions to unlock the different doors and escape down passageways. Some of them were saying distractedly that it was Xander, Xander Metzger. That he was actually here. Stella tried her best to ignore their voices and just focus on aiming, shooting, and reloading.

When the administrators were scattered in all directions, the tables were abandoned. An entire bowl of apples lay untouched in a porcelain bowl just a few yards away. Promising a better life.

Stella darted forward.

"That's her!" a familiar voice called out. His words rang clear over the gunfire and all the chaos. Stella recognized it immediately as her contact, the nurse. "That's the Ghost!"

The moment seemed to stretch, and time slowed down as her momentum pushed her forward. Away from the rest of her gang.

The nasal voice of the east administrator rang out, strangely echoed. Stella barely heard it over the pounding of her own heartbeat. "A year's supply of pills for the Ghost, dead or alive," the administrator called.

The guards who had been covering the retreat of the administrators turned around, straight into the path of the gunfire, swarming in front of her. Stella took the men out easily, but there were too many of them, more than she could shoot, and they just kept coming after her.

Behind her, her gang shouted directions, and she couldn't quite hear them. Did they need her to move? Everything was too loud. The advance guards were too close, sneering down at her.

Stella found herself grabbed by more than one set of hands, and the grips were too tight and too many, pulling in different directions. Stella tried to keep shooting, only to wrestle with the strong arms that tried to pull her Glock away from her. She told herself that it was going to be okay as she tried to slow down the racing beat of her heart. She couldn't panic; now wasn't the time. She couldn't let herself think about why they were doing this, why they wanted her so bad, and what would happen to her if she couldn't just hold it together.

Someone howled in feral rage behind her. Was that Xander? The guard grabbing her jerked and slumped down. His hold slackened.

She felt something warm spray across her, obscuring her vision in red. She tried to close her eyes and hold herself in the moment. She tried to shut out their words, which echoed through her. *"That's the Ghost! That's her!"* But it was no use. Stella felt her calm deteriorate, like water dripping out of the palm of her hand.

The memory came unbidden to her mind, and once it came, it was like an opened floodgate, rushing in, drowning her. She couldn't stop it. It had been five years ago, and she could remember it like it was happening now, all over again.

WERE THOSE FOOTSTEPS? SOMETHING WAS WRONG—THERE were too many and too in sync. When the infected ran, it was disorganized, like raindrops smacking the pavement. What was going on?

Stella peeked out of the vertical slits of the window blinds. They were in the mid-level of the skyscraper. Her dad said that it was too high for the infected to wander into, but low enough for them to run back down.

Out the window, the arches of the George Washington Bridge appeared, the rest hidden behind buildings.

Walking in the street were people. Not infected. Not the horde. She could tell by the way they walked. She hadn't seen so many in a long time. Used to be that she'd see normal people, running and chased by the infected, but not so much anymore.

Big crowds usually weren't people anymore. She was used to the hordes and the hunting cries in the night. They bothered Xander, though. He'd wake up and panic.

"Dad?" Stella called.

After a moment of silence, she called his name again, louder. "Dad?"

Stella frowned. Why wasn't he answering?

Her calls woke up Xander. He rolled out of bed and joined Stella by the windowsill, placing a hand on her shoulder. His grip tightened as he looked outside.

"Who are they?" Stella asked him.

He didn't answer at first.

He got quiet sometimes when he was afraid.

"Guards from the underground." Xander's voice sounded dried out, like everything good was sucked out of it.

More than a hundred men walked up and down the street, going into buildings.

Were they looking for food?

One man ran out of a building, an infected close behind him. The infected caught up, biting down, grasping the man with its teeth. The others worked together, bashing the infected and the bitten man both with clubs, shovels and knives. They turned them into a raw mass of thick sludge that didn't look like bodies anymore.

Then they started to point excitedly and run.

"What are they doing?" Stella asked. Seemed like they had found what they wanted. The men flocked toward it like the mutated pigeons scrambling to breadcrumbs.

Through the crowd of them, Stella couldn't see what had gotten them so excited. At least not at first.

"Dad," Stella whispered, fear spreading, weighing down her limbs until the pressure was going to make her burst. Jittery panic flowed through her, worse than anything. Worse, even, than getting bit the first time.

Her father was down there, and they had him, pulling him out into the center. Surrounding him.

Stella could see his lips moving, and the frantic gestures of his arms, but she was too far to hear his words. All she needed to see was the stiff, unyielding postures of all of those men. None of them were listening to him anyway.

They pushed her father hard until he fell to the broken asphalt. Then they attacked. A guard bashed her father in the back of the head with a club.

Stella hadn't realized that she had leapt forward until she registered the feel of arms like steel bars wrapped around her, holding her back. Even as she scratched wildly, digging into skin.

She screamed. The sound of her cries were louder, muffled against Xander's hand, trapping most of the desperate noise inside of her.

"There's too many," Xander pleaded with her. "There's nothing you can do."

Xander tried to wrestle her away from the window. But they were dragging her dad. She had to do something.

She fought as they pulled him away, as she recognized that her father didn't look right anymore. Like they hit him too hard. She fought as they took his body away and out of sight.

"Stella, please stop!"

She did.

Stella went limp and fell to the floor.

~

AFTER ALL THIS TIME, SHE STILL FOUGHT HER MEMORIES. IT was too easy to slip into that numbness where nothing mattered. She had to keep her rage at the underground city, at the guards, at the administrators; it protected her. If she couldn't summon up her anger, what was left for her to feel?

"It's going to be okay," Xander muttered in her ear. He carried her, cradled in his arms, as he ran through the tunnels.

What happened?

Her memories were a blur, and she was shaking.

Blood was smeared across her face and arms. Was it hers? Was it all from the guards?

Stopping at a storage alcove, Xander scanned the perimeter before checking on her. He looked closely at her face and blanched like he was afraid of what he saw. Then he cradled her cheek in his calloused palm.

Even though they were in the middle of the underground, in the middle of a raid, Xander leaned in and kissed her.

She closed her eyes at the touch of his soft mouth and the luscious warmth that spread through her core.

What was happening? What was he doing?

Her mind shuffled through faces. Some clear, some fading. All images of people who used to be her friends. Until Xander had decided they had gotten too close.

Stella blinked and pulled away. "Stop."

Xander dropped his gaze, swallowing. "Do I get to know why?"

Stella dragged her palm across her face, wiping away blood.

"I can't live like this. Watching you hurt people. Watching you kill people. For me." She didn't even bother to learn the names of some of the new recruits into the gang. Did anything she could to stop him from getting suspicious of the other men.

Xander buried his face into the crook of her neck and whispered, "I can't lose you."

"You weren't going to lose me to any of the men you sent off to die." Stella blinked as moisture gathered at the corners of her eyes. They were her friends.

She'd had to learn how to stop making friends.

"I'm sorry," Xander whispered, pulling back. His eyes on her lips.

Stella turned away.

Xander sighed.

Behind them, the call of guards echoed through the tunnels. Xander tightened his grip on her and continued carrying her through the tunnels.

In a hurt voice, Xander asked, "Is this because of the scientist?"

Stella paused, with a *no* on the tip of her lips. Xander couldn't change. But she needed his help to save someone. Even if it was the last time.

"Yes, this is about him. If you want me, you should let him go."

12

W hen there was work to be done, time flowed together and passed Gavin by. He had asked for a large room with access to the sun. The drained hollow of a swimming pool was perfect for what he had in mind. He disinfected the entire length of the room, scrubbing off the mixture of dust, mold, and the oily residue of the toxins, finally revealing the baby blue of the tiles underneath. Then he went through every corner of the room, sealing off all the possible toxin entrance points.

As soon as that part of the work was done, Gavin found himself alone with his thoughts. Was Stella hurt? Why couldn't he do anything to stop her from getting hurt? If she liked him, was her choice going to be taken from her? How was he going to get home? How was his work managed without him? Waiting was terrible.

He could go into his room and pick up the pistol Stella left him. From there, he could head out and look for soil to start the second part of the work.

As Gavin opened the door, he found himself staring into the barrel of a gun.

Gavin winced, holding his arms up as he took a step back from the guard blocking his exit.

"There's nothing left to do in here." Gavin pointed back to the fully disinfected room.

The man looked behind Gavin into the room and gave the now gleaming surfaces a double take. It did look much better. Light streamed through the cleaned windows, illuminating the soft blue tiles. This man wouldn't be the first to be surprised by the amount that Gavin could get done in a short time.

"I just need to get out there and start collecting some soil." Gavin jerked back as the door was shut abruptly in his face. This time, Gavin heard the click of the lock that went along with it.

He wasn't left alone for long. Gavin's door unlocked a few minutes later and Sam stepped into the room, holding a plate of vegetables that looked like they came out of a can, which he handed to Gavin.

"How did you get rid of your guard?" Sam asked him.

"He probably got tired of hearing me pacing," Gavin replied.

"You do realize that it's only eight in the morning, right?" Sam said as he looked around at the cleaned state of the room. When Gavin responded with nothing more than a shrug, Sam sighed and sat down. "Never mind."

Having nothing better to do, Gavin began to eat, wondering if these vegetables were somehow better than the others, or if he was just getting used to the taste of things here.

When Gavin finished his last green bean, Sam crossed his arms and began to speak.

"I still can't get it out of my head. What happened to Celia's gang," Sam focused on the pool tiles, a distant look in his eyes. "By the time I got there, they had already given up. One by one, it would start with someone, until they knew it would happen to them all. I saw it, and there wasn't a damn thing I could do to save them. They were together, watching their friends die. Just waiting their turn. It was the worst thing I had ever seen." Sam shook his head. "It was just like you said. Their oxygen pills blew up inside of their lungs."

"We ran tests on animals. It's not something you ever forget," Gavin explained. He couldn't bring himself to mention the factory member who had taken a bad pill. Seeing that was not something you could ever forget, either. Once heard, it could never be unheard.

"Some of them were talking to me, and I don't know if any of it was real and made sense. At that point, they didn't even ask me what I was doing there. Didn't really matter that someone had snuck in, who I was or anything like that. They were saying things like, 'He seemed like he was such a nice man,' and 'We trusted him. Why did he do this to us?'"

Gavin froze as his throat went dry. A nice man, with access to the bad pills, did this? All the evidence seemed to point to the same person. Gavin put the image of one nice man he knew out of his mind. He didn't believe it, couldn't believe it until he had all the facts.

"They weren't just killed, Gavin. They were murdered. Someone did this to them. I don't know why anyone would even want to do that. Celia's gang was different, nothing like ours. They were just scavengers, picking at everything and making trades. They never hurt anyone. I stayed with them as they died. All of them." Sam hung his head as his shoulders slumped.

"I don't know how to say this, but I actually came to thank you," Sam admitted. "As soon as you left, Xander started acting crazy. Yelling for no reason, breaking things. I knew I had to find a way out. I went to Celia's gang and got mixed with all that. I kept on thinking how I didn't have any way to keep Nat safe. She's already a couple months preg-nant. The two of us were going to be next. If you hadn't made that deal with Xander, we would be."

"I promised Natalia I'd help if I could. It's a stupid rule anyway," Gavin replied.

"I can see why Stella likes you," Sam told him matter-of-factly.

Gavin jerked his head back. Was Sam serious? He ducked his chin to hide the flush of heat creeping up the back of his neck and jaw.

"I'm not so sure that she does," he replied honestly.

"She wouldn't have tried to save you if she didn't," Sam said. "Plenty of guys have fallen in love with Stella before and she just ignored them."

"Xander's in love with her, too. He was planning on going into New York after her," Gavin said.

"How did you find out about that?" Sam asked. He didn't even bother trying to deny it.

"I heard it." Gavin left out the fact that he had heard it from Ben as the man continued trying to scare him away from Stella.

"If Stella wanted to be with Xander, it would have already happened."

He shouldn't push it, but the curiosity nagged at him. Gavin opened his mouth to ask more.

Their conversation was interrupted when the door opened again and Gavin's guard stepped in, holding out a bag.

"This is sand. I can't use this." Gavin grabbed a handful of the dried-out material and let it slip through his fingers back into the bag. "Soil will be under plants. I saw some blackened weeds that took out most of the toxins. I can show you where." Gavin was cut off as the guard turned his back on him and walked out the door.

"They're under orders not to let you out of here. The more you ask to get out, the less likely it's going to happen," Sam warned him. "I know what plants you're talking about. I'll go get some people together and bring that for you." Sam stepped back out of the room.

A half hour or so passed before Sam and the others returned, carrying bags of soil. Real—albeit dry—soil. It would work. Gavin set to work checking the soil, dispersing the toxins within and using heat to get the rest out of it, as Sam and the others left to fetch more. They continued in that cycle for hours—Sam and the men digging up soil and bringing it back, and Gavin filtering the toxins out of it. Now that Gavin was under the rhythm and spell of work, time slipped by again.

The pool was already halfway filled with soil by the time the gang members who had gone on the raids returned. They walked into the room and deposited the tools and things they had collected on the floor. Some of them looked around, surprised at the changes in the room, or walked close to the hollow where the soil was beginning to go curiously. But Gavin was more interested in the ones who looked dazed, the ones who were sporting injuries that were either visibly bandaged or hidden somewhere out of view. It appeared that the raids were not as simple and organized as he had thought. It looked like the raids, like everything else out here, had the potential to go very wrong.

When Gavin finally saw her again, she looked fine. He knew that with Stella, appearances meant very little. He had seen her just a couple of minutes after she had been attacked and brutally bitten by an infected and she had acted like nothing was wrong then, either. All of the pain, the stress, and the trauma of the experience were hidden completely away. Gavin just wanted a chance to talk to her, to make sure she was all right.

She avoided his gaze. Something must have happened. As Stella entered the room, Xander followed in close after her. Gavin didn't know what that was supposed to mean. Was she injured? Did Xander say something to her?

Xander grabbed his satchel and reached inside. All eyes were on him as he pulled out two peaches, a handful of strawberries, and some bruised yet plump red apples, placing the fruit down gently next to the other tools.

"So you did manage to get the fruit," Stella said.

Things must have really gone wrong if Stella returned without even knowing whether her part in the raid was successful or not. Gavin tried to gauge whether she looked emotionally affected, but it was difficult. She definitely didn't have the small traces of humor she usually showed. It was too hard, though, studying her as she ignored him. Gavin looked away.

"Did you want one?" Xander handed Stella one of the apples.

She looked at it curiously, picking up the apple and twirling it in her palm, before shaking her head no.

She tossed it back to Xander. "Better to save it and grow it."

Xander took the fruit back. "You sure? You're the only one out here who's never had fruit at least once."

Gavin didn't have to look her way to know that she would silently refuse. Stella would never give in to a moment of pleasure if it risked their safety.

"So you'll be able to use this?" Xander asked him, looking at the assortment of tools and fruit taken in the raid.

Gavin looked it all over. "This should work."

But his mind was still processing what could have happened in the raid.

Stella was skilled at hiding pain. Except that now she was quiet. Too quiet. She was avoiding him purposefully. That couldn't have been the result of something he'd done —he'd been here. Something must have happened when she and Xander were alone together.

Gavin ground his teeth at the thought of Xander putting Stella at risk just to get her away from another man.

"Tomorrow, then, we'll organize some groups to get the metals and other supplies," Xander announced before pulling his things together and leaving.

Having dropped off everything, the other gang members began to quietly file out of the room, off to do whatever other things they had to do—nurse wounds and eat, go back to their rooms and just fall asleep. Gavin half expected Stella to stay, to let him know what had happened and what to expect next. But when the others left the swimming room, Stella joined them. She left without a word—without even a glance his way.

13

Stella walked down a corridor lined with numbered doors and knocked on a wood panel with the knuckle of her finger. There was the sound of a latch turning from within, then Nat opened the door wide to let her in.

Stella eased a drawstring bag off her shoulders, opening it to reveal her haul—painkillers, bandages, antibiotics. Even a baby bottle. It was a good thing plastic never decomposed. The plastic goods out there would likely outlast them all. She laid out each item on Nat's table, lining them up with care.

"You don't have to keep scavenging for me." Natalia scooped up the pills and stashed them in a drawer, along with the others Stella had gathered for her. "I'm pregnant, not on my deathbed. Besides, I've got months to go."

Natalia pressed her hand against her mostly flat stomach. As she was wearing a loose shirt, it was like nothing had changed at all. But one of the first things Stella had brought back from scavenging was a pregnancy test. The double lines confirmed it. Natalia's life was about to get more complicated.

"Xander's had teams scavenging for days. It'd be stupid not to look for medicine too."

"You grabbed this right under Xander's nose?" Nat held up the baby bottle, and smirked when Stella nodded. "He'd lose his mind if he saw that."

"He's already lost his mind." Stella muttered, without thinking.

Natalia placed the bottle back down carefully. "And you?"

"What about me?"

"Where's your mind at?"

Stella shook her head. "I don't even know."

The longer she avoided Gavin, the more she thought of him. She would be rummaging through a deserted house, searching for metal in the form of necklaces and pots and electronics, when she'd remember the blush on Gavin's face the first time she saw him, or the little smile when she held his hand. Every day she thought things were going to get easier, and every day she realized she was wrong.

"Sam says you aren't talking to Gavin anymore. Is that what you want?"

"No." Stella pressed her eyes closed and shook her head. What she wanted? She couldn't have what she wanted. Not if it meant putting the people she cared about at risk.

"Stella." Natalia reached out and held her hand. "Don't do this to yourself."

"I have to." Stella said in a dull voice. "I don't have a choice. He's not safe around me."

"Why? Because of Xander?"

As Stella nodded, Natalia squeezed her hand.

"I know what you did for me. The trade underground to get medicine." Natalia pointed to the drawer filled with scavenged medical supplies. "You keep risking your life. You can't keep helping people if you destroy yourself in the process. Right now, it sounds like you're making the wrong choice for the right reasons and pretending it isn't the wrong choice. "

"I don't know what else to do. I can't take seeing another person I care about die. Because of me."

She'd made her bargain with Xander. Now she'd just have to live with it. How else could she get Gavin home? Getting him through hordes of the infected was one thing. But the underground city? The administrators were out for her blood. Now, she could never take him back. Not on her own.

Natalia pulled Stella into a hug, holding her tight. Leaning in close, Natalia whispered, "Whatever you do, make sure it is the right choice for you. Take care of yourself for once."

Do something for herself?

If nothing else, she'd see him one last time. Even if it was only to say a last goodbye.

This wasn't Gavin's home. He came from a different world. He didn't belong out here. With her. Getting him home always meant letting him go.

14

The work was much the same thing that Gavin would have done back at the factory. He was checking the levels of the soil and assembling the project. He lay down with his back touching the warm soil as he worked under the machine. The air purification machine would be the first thing he assembled.

Working here, he could almost imagine he was back at home, back at the oxygen factory. He was busy; he was doing what he knew. Except that if he concentrated, he wouldn't be able to see the occasional shape of a massive sea creature out beyond the boundary. He could only see yellow skies, listless clouds, and the disfigured silhouette of mutated pigeons.

Gavin melted down the metals that came to him from the different raids in the form of everything from old women's jewelry to battered traffic signs, and kitchen utensils like stainless steel pots and pans and iron skillets. He separated the piles into the three sorts of metals he would need: copper, iron, and steel.

Gavin couldn't help but notice that whenever there was

a plan for people to get more parts, Xander always paired himself with Stella. He tried not to notice that when the two of them went anywhere, they always walked together. Stella still hadn't spoken to him since they had come back from New York City.

So Gavin just retreated back into his work and tried his best not to think about it.

He had almost lost track of the days, just settling into a pattern of work, watching the machine grow and take shape under his experienced hands. He molded each piece of melted-down metal like he would have done back home at the factory, interlaced with wires and forged with connections.

When it came to machines, things made sense. Sometimes people around him would do things he couldn't understand, things that had no flow or logic to them. People could just hurt one another, and he didn't know why. Like Stella. She just stopped talking to him, right when he had thought that they had a connection. Now he didn't know what he was going to do about it.

The world of machines, on the other hand, made sense to him. He could look at something and figure out how it was put together—the wires, the metal embedded in the wires, the positive and negative flow of electricity. All of it was something that could be broken down and understood. Machines, no matter what they were built for, all followed the same basic principles. Once he understood one of those principles, he could apply it to them all. He wished that people were the same way. He missed Stella.

Gavin worked on the machine late into the night. The fact that the others had already fallen asleep wasn't important. He was so close to finishing that he could taste it. If he stopped now, he would face a sleepless night thinking about what little he needed to do to have a working machine. It would eat at him until the morning.

Focused on work, he didn't notice at first that he wasn't alone.

He didn't hear anything, but rather felt the eyes on him, watching him. Gavin glanced up from his place on his back and looked into her beautiful violet eyes—the rich purple surrounded by those snowy white lashes. She was simply lovely at first glance, with her face arranged into an expression of easy confidence. There was a quiet, flickering sense of power radiating from her presence, underlying her every movement. The slender curves of her face contrasted sharply with her short, cropped hair, and Gavin couldn't help but imagine what it would look like if it was longer, if those delicate white strands were allowed to grow and fall in waves, contrasting against the deep violet.

Gavin forced himself to look away from her, turning back to the machine. He could remember every touch. He could remember the way her slender hands felt against his own. He could remember how he held her, protecting her against the infected. Even in his arms, she was the one with the power to protect him.

He tried to put her presence out of his mind, to forget the stories that she had shared with him, forget the time in the van after all of those infected had charged them down. All the times that he thought nothing would stop him from death, she was there—scaring off the infected, finding a hiding place, always prepared, coming up with a solution and keeping the two of them alive. He remembered those words she had said to him in the van.

"You trusted your instincts in there, and you saved my life. I don't know why you doubt yourself. I will never come back to this

*city again. Never. Unless it's with you. I wouldn't want anyone
else beside me."*

Then she had leaned in closer to him and stared at his
lips. Gavin remembered how every muscle in his body had
tensed and how his thoughts cleared out of his head, leaving
him completely aware and transfixed by her presence.
Nothing existed in the entire world except her. He was sure
that after everything they had been through, they were
about to kiss. He had never felt closer to anyone else before,
had never let anyone else in. Stella was different. But now he
was just left thinking that he was wrong.

He didn't ask her what had happened in the underground city; he didn't need to hear all the details. But there
was just one thing he had to know. He had to ask it.

"Are you in a relationship with Xander?" Gavin tightened a screw on the machine. He didn't look at her and kept
working instead.

"No," Stella replied, sounding tired.

"He wants you. Everybody knows it." Gavin checked the
wires.

"Yes, he does."

"Do you want to be with him?" Gavin asked.

Stella paused before she answered, and Gavin's heart
rate sped up.

"I've known him since he was just twelve years old,
before he started up the gang. We've been through a lot
together."

Already, Gavin could feel his heart sinking in his chest.
It sounded like an explanation on her part, and he didn't
want to hear it. He had been wrong, and it was as simple as
that. He had gone to a new place for the first time and met
someone amazing. But the truth was that it had been just
too good to be true. He had seen more than what was there.

"So you do." Though his hands were still on the machine, they were no longer moving. Gavin tried to show the same level of calm that he had shown since the beginning of their conversation, despite the fact that everything was different now. Stella would never be with him. He didn't know what he was going to do without her.

"Xander was the first friend I ever had. In all the time I've known him, all I wanted was to be his friend. But that's not good enough for him," Stella admitted.

Gavin waited, preparing for the truth, knowing he needed to hear it even if the words weren't what he wanted.

"He's found a way to get rid of every guy who has ever been interested in me and killed the ones he couldn't scare away," Stella said.

Gavin stopped what he was doing, staring at Stella with wide eyes.

"If I cared about you at all, I would stay away from you," Stella whispered.

"If you want to be with me, then be with me," Gavin disagreed, finding his voice.

Stella pressed her lips together in a slight grimace. "You don't know him like I do. I've known Xander longer than anyone else here. Why do you think I don't want to be with him?"

"Well, then, what are you going to do?" Gavin said. "Are you going to end up with him? You can't just keep him waiting forever."

"I can't be with you if it ends with you getting hurt. I can't see someone else I care about die."

"I'm a little harder to kill than you think. I've dealt with people like Xander before. Trust me."

Stella shook her head slowly, biting her lip as if she were

nervous. "You don't know what you have gotten yourself into here. It's really not that simple."

"Just give me a little bit of time. Maybe I'll find a way to change your mind." Gavin returned to the machine, checking the last few connections before closing the lid, hearing it snap shut. "It's ready. Do you want to see if it works?"

Stella stared at the machine curiously and nodded.

Gavin flipped the switch to the little machine and listened as it hummed into life, softly churning out a constant stream of sound when before there was only quiet. The purification machine worked as he knew it would work. But that wasn't the moment of truth. He knew the real test was what was to come.

It had never been done before. No one had ever tried to create oxygen pills above ground. But at the same time, as soon as Xander had asked him, Gavin couldn't help but be intrigued. That was one of the last projects he had been working on in the oxygen factory before ending up here— planting the seaweed that could survive in the open ocean outside of the oxygen factory. He held up the vial he had brought with him. There was so little of it left. If he was wrong, if he had made a mistake, there was no backup plan.

Gavin grasped the apple from the ledge surrounding the edge of the pool, undisturbed for the last few days. He had run tests on all the fruits and found that this one would work. He only had one chance; he had to make it count.

Gavin concentrated, steadying himself as he placed the apple on the ground and covered it with a thin layer of soil. He had calculated it carefully, purifying water earlier in the day and drenching the soil with just the right amount. He took a look at the vial in his pocket that had a handful of drops stubbornly clinging to the bottom of the glass. Why hadn't he bothered to bring more with him that day? Why had he used so much of it? What would he do if it didn't work? It wasn't as if it would be easy to convince them to let him take a stroll into the shipment station and place his supply request. He flicked at the chemical compound in the vial, watching the solid green liquid swirl about in the glass.

Gavin dropped to his knee and carefully hovered right over the spot where he had lightly buried the apple. With steady hands, Gavin dropped two fat green drops right over the spot. Then he got to his feet quick, stoppering the vial as he went. Gavin leaned away, staring as those drops beaded on top of the soil, until the surface tension broke and they sank down into the dirt.

He knew it worked the moment the sturdy little bud poked its way through the dirt, unwinding upward toward the light. He tried to stop himself from smiling at the little bud, trying to be scientific and professional about the whole thing, while inside he wanted to scream and holler that they had done it, they had done it. The compound he had created didn't work just on seaweed after all.

Stella leaned in for a closer look. Gavin collected her in his arms carefully and pulled her out of the way. They weren't done here, not by a long shot.

For a moment, the little green sprout remained a tiny bud on the ground as it gathered nutrients and soaked up the rest of the chemicals from the vial. Then slowly, almost cautiously, the bud began to writhe its way upward. It thickened and darkened as its outside became coated in bark.

Then, rushing upward, the tree took form. It rose high, the branches spreading skywards. All they could hear was the rustling of growing and the rumbling under their feet as roots snaked through the earth, spreading under the dirt as the tree pushed its way higher.

Dots of green beaded across the branches before uncoiling and emerging as leaves. All around the leaves, pink-tipped, pale flowers blossomed into a brief existence until the petals began to fall, one by one to the ground, plump red fruit swelling up in their place. Within a couple of minutes, the bud was gone, and what stood in its place was a full-fledged apple tree.

Gavin reached up and picked one of the apples from a lower branch of the tree, handing it to her. As Stella took the apple, her fingers brushed against his wrist—the warmth of her touch spread through him. She smiled as she lifted the red fruit to her lips. Tasting it in one big bite, her eyes never left his.

15

The leaves rustled in the light breeze of the air purifier. Standing under the newly grown apple tree that had been seeds and dirt moments before, Stella could hardly remember why she'd stayed away.

Gavin released three of the little hummingbird machines and they flitted about the room, harvesting oxygen pills into a little pile at the base of the tree. She had expected him to be angry with her, and she had been ready to tell him the truth—that getting close to Xander was the best way she could think to protect him, maybe even to get him home. She hadn't expected his calm questions, his kindness. She hadn't expected this.

She bit into the apple again and tasted why Gavin had had to hide all of those repulsed faces whenever he was given anything to eat that had ever been frozen or stored in a can. The fruit was sweet and crisp. Stella hadn't known food could be so good.

Stella finished the apple with a few more bites, savoring each one. She looked up when she was done to find Gavin watching her with a half-smile on his face, almost like he was trying to hide it.

"I'll take that," he said, gesturing to the core. "Seeds and stuff."

Right. Stella handed him the core and he placed it on a table, watching her all the while. She looked up at the tree, fighting laughter. It had been so long since she'd seen any kind of plant that wasn't dead or dying, and this was a far cry from that. This was life, beyond any of her wildest expectations.

"This is what you do?" she said in wonder. "Back at the factory?"

"Kind of." Gavin raked a hand through his hair. "But this... This is a first."

A damn good first. And, judging by the oxygen pills piling up, it was working.

Light streamed down, striking the leaves into a radiant overlapping pattern of green. Brimming with life. There was nothing else like it out here. Nothing like that texture of delicate veins, nothing like the red promise of the apples that hung in clusters, all plump and round.

Xander wouldn't see it that way. Stella could emulate that same cool calculation, that same desire for rules and order, which dominated Xander's thoughts and colored his perception. This tree wouldn't be just a tree for Xander. It was power. What was more, keeping its creator wrapped under his little thumb would be another source of power. Stella had run out of time to think about this. She left Gavin, with an explanation that wasn't an explanation. "There's something that I have to do."

STELLA ALWAYS KNEW WHERE XANDER WAS STAYING. IN THE beginning, Xander would take rooms on the middle floors, following the precautions her father had laid out. But after years of safety, building up the most powerful and feared gang outside the underground city, Xander now took rooms in the penthouse suite.

Stella rapped her knuckles lightly against the door and listened to the quiet stride of his footsteps as he opened the door. He didn't look surprised to see her. No one else would stop by so late. Most of the other gang members avoided him; they hadn't spent years knowing him before he took charge and set out the rules, before he became driven with the need to survive out here.

"Hey, there," Xander said in a quiet voice he used just when he was talking to her. Xander reached out for her, brushing one of his hands against her cheek. "What's wrong, couldn't sleep again?"

"I just wanted to see you, to thank you." Stella let his hand linger and let him get distracted. "I never thanked you before. You saved me again."

"You know that I always look out for you."

"I know," Stella replied with a faint trace of a smile hiding behind her serious expression.

"I care about you," Xander said.

It was true. Even if she was the only person in the entire world that Xander cared about, it was true.

"So what happens next?" Stella placed her hand on top of Xander's.

"What do you mean?"

"I've never done anything like this before," Stella murmured, leaning her head against Xander's palm. "It seems like that machine will be finished soon. Once he's gone, it'll just be you and me again."

"He's a fast worker," Xander mused. "Just imagine it. With that machine, we'll never have to worry about oxygen pills again. I get it now, why you brought him here."

"Yes, he's done a lot for us."

"Maybe he wouldn't mind doing just one more project. Maybe you could ask him."

"I'll talk to him," Stella said, the smile frozen on her face as she fought to keep her tone calm and collected.

"You've been a good friend to him. He might even want to stick around for you, at least a little while longer," Xander added with a smirk as he bent down closer to her. Stella realized he was about to kiss her at the same moment she knew she didn't want him to.

Stella pulled away, looking down at her feet shyly. "It's getting late," she whispered. She kept her head down so she wouldn't have to see the disappointed look he would try to hide from her as she wished him goodnight.

Stella calmly left Xander's apartment, but as soon as she was out of earshot, she began to jog. It seemed like after all he had said, Xander was going back on his word. With each step she took away from Xander's room, the more times she turned the idea around and around in her head, the more certain she grew. Xander was never going to let him go.

So now what? How was she going to get him home?

Stella could picture Gavin, the best person she had ever known, being manipulated and used. He might as well have just died out there in the desert sand for all the good she had done him. Every day of the rest of Gavin's life, Xander would quietly increase the security, until he became little more than a prisoner. Would she be able to live with herself, knowing that she had let it happen?

Her time for indecision was over. Her quick footsteps

took her back to the swimming room, and her mind had to make time to catch up.

There was only Ben, the guard on duty, who stood between her and Gavin. Ben was looking his age tonight, with deep lines around the eyes he strained to keep open. Even now, Ben eased against the hallway wall until he was leaning against it in comfort, close to drifting off. Stella didn't want to take any risks.

"Hey, Ben," she said quietly.

His eyes snapped open and his hands darted to his holster at his side before he realized who was speaking.

"Stella." Ben returned the greeting with a nod.

Stella approached him slowly, idly sliding her fingers along the hallway panels until her hand came to a rest by the fire extinguisher. "You aren't one I'd picture out here so late."

"I have to wait for the scientist," Ben said, straining to keep his voice from sounding tired.

"How's he doing with that machine?" Stella asked him.

"Not sure." Ben rubbed a knuckle under his eye, trying to wake himself.

"Why's that?"

"Xander gave me specific instructions not to disturb him while he's working," Ben replied dutifully. Stella guessed he was stating the procedures word for word.

"That's perfect," she murmured.

Before Ben's sleep-fogged mind could process what Stella just said, she gripped the fire extinguisher and swung it in a clean arc. She felt the clang reverberate throughout the hollow metal canister as it hit Ben in the side of his head. Ben dropped to the ground.

Stella returned the extinguisher to its place on the wall.

She pressed lightly against the crook of Ben's neck and felt the pulsing of his heartbeat. She dragged him around the corner, arranging his unconscious body comfortably. He would probably wake up with the worst headache of his life, but he would wake. He would get some rest for now, at least. But Xander was going to give him hell for what she was about to do.

Stella drummed her fist against the door to get Gavin's attention, and when she opened it, there he was. All he did was stare straight into her eyes, which must have looked half crazed with determination.

"Come with me," Stella said. She didn't have to say anything more.

It wasn't until they were in the front lobby with Stella gripping the doorknob, hesitating, that Gavin finally questioned her. "What are we doing?"

"Something crazy," she answered, hoping that it was just crazy enough to work.

On sleepless nights, she would watch them, staring out from behind the safety of the window. She would watch their typical movements and their kill patterns. It was all just knowledge she never thought she would actually use.

Stella could remember some of those nights where she had stood watching the infected tear their prey, eating at it until there was nothing left. From the time when they were young, Xander would only be able to look out the window at night for a few minutes before he had to turn away again to hide his fear. Stella knew Xander would never risk going out in the darkness. She knew it might be their only chance to escape.

"We're going out there," Stella said. "I'll do what I can to get you back home."

Gavin didn't back down, though he had seen up close

what the infected were capable of when they came out at night. "Do you think we have a chance?"

"Back before all the survivors moved to the underground, I couldn't tell you how many people got killed at night. It was the panic that did it, the screaming. We have a chance to make it if we stay silent."

"Is this like the rules for surviving in the city? If we see an infected, we kill them silently?" Gavin asked, with no trace of indecision.

"Too dangerous to kill them in the dark. The best you can hope for is to be quiet enough that they don't notice you. No talking, no noise at all. We're stepping into their world now." Stella tightened her grip on the doorknob as she spoke. She embraced the tight press of metal, needing that solid contact. She knew it was her last safe moment until it was all over, and it was hard to let go.

She twisted it open, and they left.

Outside, she could hear them immediately, too many to pick out where exactly they all were. Gavin's footsteps fell silent behind her as he heard them, too. She reached behind her and slipped her fingers in between his, letting the warmth of those calloused hands reassure her that they were together and they were alive.

Gavin gripped her hand tight when one of the infected shrieked out its hunting cry, but he managed to restrain from any audible reaction. Stella could hear the pounding of bare feet running against sand, but she couldn't tell if they were approaching or running off into the distance.

She forced herself to keep at an easy pace and not to panic. She walked straight ahead, visualizing their path as her eyes slowly adjusted to the deep darkness. She forced herself to maintain that slow pace, even as she could make out their shapes around them, those darker patches drifting through the night.

The infected held her full attention. The best chance they had depended on her being able to watch the infected and avoid them. It was useless to wish they had those shirts now. She had pulled shirts off dead infected so it would hide their scent. It would do them no good to think about what would happen if the infected caught their human scent and closed ranks around them. The best Stella could do was to keep her calm and influence Gavin to do the same.

Stella squeezed Gavin's hand back hard as she felt a tremor under their feet. That faint rumbling grew into a steady beat, and this sound was too heavy to be footfalls made by human bodies. But then the rumbling grew distinct enough for Stella to know that it was coming straight at them. The sound grew clearer until she could hear the clatter of hooves biting into the sand. This couldn't be happening.

Stella tugged on Gavin's hand to get his attention before she gripped down on his hand hard and began to sprint. Adrenaline flooded through her as they ran, until she could barely feel her muscles strain or her heart pound. In the rush of movement, Stella felt a magnified awareness, as if all the details had sharpened into crisp points. All she could see was each dark outline of the infected around them and how many of them seemed to turn their way.

Their path should have been clear, would have been clear, but out of all the empty spaces, they had to come to this one.

Stella saw the animals from time to time on their mad dash to escape through the hordes of infected, on their constant routes to the black grasses that barely had time to poke their spiked leaves through desert sand before they were eaten back down.

Running behind Gavin and Stella was the deer herd. Seen in the light, some of them had four legs, while others had five or more. Most of them were covered in boils and claw marks from the infected. Now all Stella knew was their approaching bodies as the faster ones overtook them. In spite of Stella and Gavin's mad dash, the herd had begun to close in around them.

Stella didn't dare say a word to Gavin, not out here, not in the darkness. All she could do was clench on to his hand and keep up their furious pace and hope that he understood. They had to keep running. They had to stay silent, hidden in the center of the herd. All those warm, running bodies would draw the infected from miles around, and there was nothing else to do but run amidst them. They ran even as she felt grime-encrusted fur brush against her arm.

Stella felt a new jolt of adrenaline surge through her body at the first sounds of the shrieks. These shrieks quickly turned into the sounds of struggling and dying bellows as a doe was dragged away from the others. The sound would draw in any infected that couldn't already hear the sharp patter of hundreds of hooves on the run.

Stella could see hands reaching out all around them: pale five-fingered flesh equipped with the ragged edges of never-filed nails and smudged with the grime of previous hunts. Stella maneuvered them the best she could into the center of the running herd, cringing inside each time she saw another hand reach out toward them.

For the first time, she didn't think about the strength of the oxygen pill in her lungs. She didn't think about holding back to make sure she had the strength to run straight to the underground city. The only thought on her mind was just keeping up, just making it now and ensuring she wasn't the one tangled in nails, ripped to the ground to be eaten alive.

They ran as the buck to their right went down, bleating in a furious struggle to live. Stella muscled her way deeper into the herd, surrounding herself and Gavin by a furred wall of deer, far away from the bucking and thrashing of that desperate animal. As the sound of struggles quieted, Stella knew they had finished him.

The herd moved as one, turning sharply out of the way of a building and following the curve of the road. Stella turned along with them, seeing the building ahead and anticipating the change. The sharp movement coupled with the sweat from their combined exertions was just enough to wrench Gavin's hand out of her own.

Stella continued to run for a moment, rocked forward by momentum, before she reached behind to take Gavin's hand once more. She felt nothing. There was no one there. Frantically, she pivoted, looking for him.

Stella had stopped running completely, seeking him out. She stood stock still as the deer veered out of her way with nimble precision. He wasn't anywhere. Every human figure around reached out for her with blind, infected eyes.

Stella stood frozen with indecision. She bit down hard on her lip to stop herself from screaming out his name as panic clouded her judgment. She strained to hear if they had gotten to him already. Was he fighting them? Where? What could she do?

A human hand latched on to her shoulder, pulling her back firmly, and she had to fight down the scream that wanted to tear its way out of her throat. She whirled around, ready to kill, just to find Gavin's face there instead, his kind eyes laced with worry.

Before she had time to do something completely stupid,

like cry out his name or lean forward and kiss him right here, in the middle of a stampede, Gavin swung her right off her feet and into his arms.

He took off, gaining back some of the ground they had lost. Stella leaned against his chest, listening to the hammering beat of his heart as he sprinted. Even holding her, Gavin began to regain lost ground. Watching the world stream by, surrounded by muscled arms, Stella realized Gavin was holding back. He was a lot stronger than she had thought.

He ran until less of the infected raised their hands against them, the numbers dropping off with each successful kill.

When Gavin was sure that none of the infected were running after the herd, he slowed his run down to a jog, letting the rest of the herd run on to seek their pastures. As the noise of the deer passed off into the distance, the two were left in silence.

Gavin slowed to a halt, bending to let her down. When her feet touched earth, Stella didn't move away. Instead, she leaned against him, pulling him tight against her in a fierce hug. She burrowed her face right in the crook of his neck, feeling the heat of his skin against the night chill.

There was still danger all around them, but here with him, Stella felt safe. She didn't want to think about what would happen after she took him back to the oxygen factory. He was here, and he was safe for now. Stella held him close before taking his hand in hers and setting back on course to the underground city.

16

G avin watched her raise the lid with caution, letting sand drift off slowly, revealing the entrance to the underground city. The two of them stared into the depths uncovered, and Gavin couldn't help but feel that the way into the underground looked like a darker pit than anything else out in the night.

Walking down the curving iron staircase out of the scant moonlight, the air became chilled and dank against his skin. Descending those stairs felt nothing like stepping into a new city that could sustain a number of human lives. This was a tunnel, buried deep under the earth.

Now he understood Stella's grim expression every time that she mentioned the underground city. Gavin wasn't just walking into danger, but getting suffocated by it. The walls were tight as they entered the tunnels, distancing themselves from the latch that served as the only entrance and exit.

The light sound of their footsteps resounded in the hallway. Gavin looked to the end of the narrow corridor to the little he could see around the bend, wondering if there were any people around. How could people live confined like this? Who wouldn't want to escape from this place?

"No one's out now besides the night watch," Stella said in a soft voice. It was the first time either of them had spoken since they were back with her gang. "Should be quiet for the next few hours. But if we get spotted by the wrong person, we're going to have to run, or fight. This city is like a giant maze. If we get separated, just remember that all the tunnels lead to the supply room. From there, you're just a steel door and two guards away from the shipment station."

The shipment station. Having been so focused on surviving, he hadn't considered what would happen next. He was close to getting back home. But then what would happen after Stella brought him to the shipment station? Would he ever see her again? Was he ready to let her go?

Stella prowled through the corridor, keeping close to the wall with one hand casually poised near the holster at her side, ready for danger.

The cold air clung tighter to him. The low ceilings and solid walls were too close, trapping him in. Gavin shook his head. It was just in his mind that there wasn't enough space.

He had to snap out of it and focus. They weren't out of danger yet.

At first, the only sound Gavin could hear was the light tread of his boots over the static hum of fluorescent lights. The city was so quiet that he could hear the swish of fabric as he moved and the dripping of water off pipes. Then, he heard something. Stella paused, motionless, her focus on a point up ahead.

A brawny voice echoed through the hallway. "If they haven't sent it by now, it's not going to happen. What do they expect us to find?"

A second voice answered, unsettlingly close. "Nothing like this has happened before. Obviously, the administrators have no idea what to do about it."

"Keep your voice down if you're going to say things like that," the first voice snapped.

Before Gavin had time to make sense of the conversation, Stella jerked his shoulder back, pulling him down a side corridor.

Passing the same spot where Stella and Gavin just stood a moment before were two men. From their height and muscle mass to the batons strapped to their belts, to the stoic expressions on their faces, these were men who lived in violence. Gavin understood the danger on a primal level, the same as he could look at a rattlesnake or jaguar and just know.

As their footsteps faded off down the tunnels, Stella leaned into his ear and whispered, "Those are the advance guard. Stay away from them."

Gavin didn't need the warning, but he appreciated the way Stella lingered near, close to him.

He couldn't imagine himself in the shipment station, turning around to say goodbye to her. Parting ways on their separate journeys home—he'd go to the oxygen factory, while she faced these narrow passageways alone.

How could he say everything he felt? With her, he had escaped death time and time again. He didn't have words for what she meant to him.

Gavin turned and pulled Stella into a hug. His anxiety melted away with the warmth of her touch. His head drifted to rest at the crook of her neck as her arms wrapped around him. He didn't want to let her go. From Stella's tight embrace, he guessed she felt the same. All he needed was one moment longer to forget.

Soon he'd be ready to run and face down death again. Soon, he'd face the likelihood that he'd never see her again. Just for now, he forgot everything, imagining instead that they were safe.

At the sound of marching, the two of them broke apart.

"Something happened," Stella whispered. There were more footsteps than the paltry night watch Stella had described.

Gavin thought back to the conversation between the two advance guards. *If they haven't sent it by now...*

"What day is it today?" Gavin asked, comprehension dawning on him.

"Monday night," Stella replied.

Tonight was the night after shipments came in. He hadn't given enough thought to what was happening back at the oxygen factory.

"Guards aren't usually out now," Stella said. "They should mostly be asleep. They all have day shifts overseeing the cargo."

"Then what would the guards do if the shipments didn't come?" Gavin asked.

"The shipments always come on Monday," Stella replied automatically, before she paused and her tone grew cautious. "Why wouldn't it come? You think they didn't send it?"

"They might not have. Not if they were busy looking for me," Gavin replied. His father was so overprotective of him. Gavin couldn't even imagine what he had been going through for this past week.

Stella was quiet for a moment, considering. "The shipments have always come. They've come every Monday since before I was born. People won't know what to think, they'll panic."

"There's no need for that, we can just ship it out later," Gavin replied.

"Yes, but nobody here knows that. No one but you," Stella said. Her voice trailed off as the thud of footsteps became too loud to ignore.

They froze when an intense light shone directly in their faces, blinding them.

"Told you I heard something."

Gavin tensed. That was the voice of the advanced guard. His eyes strained to adjust and see around the high-powered flashlight that burned past his eyes, clawing at the back of his mind. The light glared red behind his eyelids when he shut his eyes for a moment, and he forced them open again. They wanted him disoriented. He wasn't going to let them throw him off.

Gavin focused on their feet, the only thing he could make out through the glare. The men were approaching. They wanted to get into position, to corner him, get him vulnerable. Beside him, Gavin heard Stella shifting her stance, ready to spring into action.

"He's a big one. Must think he's tough, coming down here. Thinks he can just come down for a raid, take what's ours. You think he's as strong as he looks?"

Gavin couldn't let their insults distract him as he focused on their movements.

"Forget him. Look at the girl." The advance guard spoke in a faint whisper, but not quite soft enough. After a week of living out among the infected, where sound was a death sentence, the words echoed in Gavin's mind.

Besides, Gavin didn't like the leer in the man's voice when he spoke about Stella.

"She must be that albino's daughter."

Didn't Stella say that the administrators would do

anything for a cure? Gavin could recall the exact numb look on Stella's face when she told him, *"My father didn't just die. He was murdered."*

If Stella had heard what the guards had said, she showed no sign of it. She stood motionless.

Gavin watched as the advance guards shifted their angle, trying to cut him off from Stella. They were just a few steps away from reaching her, and Stella stood stock-still.

Then Gavin charged, slamming straight into the guard, knocking him to the wall.

A stunned moment followed. They all paused and watched the guard's body hit the wall awkwardly and collapse on the ground.

Stella and the remaining advance guard reacted at the same time. Stella pivoted and ran. The other guard turned and punched Gavin hard. Gavin rolled his body back with the momentum of the punch, and as the guard lifted his fists into a fighting stance, anticipating the retaliating blow, Gavin ignored him. He raced down the full length of the hallway, pushing himself hard. He caught up with her just as she turned sharply down a side passageway.

Gavin ran with her as she weaved her way through the empty corridors and side passageways. They entered one alley and blew past a lone guard so fast that he barely had time to register who they were before they were around the bend.

Does she have a plan? Or is she reacting like a cornered animal, moving in random patterns and putting distance between herself and danger?

He didn't know.

No matter where they ran, there was only one exit. Unless they could reach it, they were trapped. They couldn't keep running forever.

Shouts and footsteps echoed through the tunnels. There were more of them, and they were after Stella. He was sure of it.

They ran until Stella reached a door that looked the same as all the others and skidded to a stop. Gavin almost ran past her and lost her. His heart drummed, pumping adrenaline through his veins. What she was up to?

Stella reached beneath her tank top and lifted a key that dangled from a simple chain around her neck. She lifted the chain over her head, placing the brass key into Gavin's hands.

"Go straight through until you find a steel door. This key will unlock it and get you to the shipment station."

Gavin saw resolve in Stella's eyes, and he didn't trust it. "You're going out there alone?"

"Gavin, it's the only way you can get back home," Stella said.

"What about you?"

Without pause, Stella closed the space between the two of them and kissed him. Gavin felt a surge of fierce determination behind those soft lips, and he let himself get lost in it. Warmth burned through him as his heart raced for her.

When Stella pulled away, Gavin took a step back, stunned.

"Promise me. You have to promise me that you'll make it there," she said.

Gavin nodded, not knowing what else he could say.

"Go." Stella pushed him in the direction of the door. "I'll distract them."

Then she ran, without a single look back.

He was alone. The passageways around him were empty now. He listened to the footsteps of Stella and the guards until the sound became too distant for him to hear. Gavin looked at the little brass key Stella had pressed into his hands. He wanted to chase after her. He needed to know she was okay. But the weight of the promise he had made to her stopped him. Gavin turned and made his way to the shipment station.

17

S tella told herself that Gavin was safe now. She had given him a chance to escape.

All it had taken was her freedom.

They'd caught her.

She forced herself to look up, staring into the eyes of the men who had killed her father.

Their beady eyes were fixed on her. Those eyes stared at her with hunger, and a shiver coursed its way over her skin.

She looked back at her feet, her determination fading in the face of their unnatural gazes. She was on stage at the administrators' lounge, surrounded by murderers. Though her glance was brief, it was enough to count them and to know that all of them were here. From the administrator of maintenance, to the administrator of shipments, all of them were here.

All along her arms, Stella could feel aches that were already blossoming into angry purple bruises, dark against her pale skin. She ignored the pain, reminding herself instead that it was nothing but a sign that she hadn't made this easy for them. They had bound her hands together, even with all the guards in the crowds, and with more lined up along the hallways outside. It was one eighteen-year-old girl against hundreds of men, and they still had taken the precaution of tying her hands together. The administrators definitely viewed her as a threat, even now. But this time, she wasn't going to get away.

So this was how it would all end. Not from the toxins in the open air or from a life of scavenging. Not from the infected who tried to hunt her down for years. This was her ending: here, under the bright stage lights, and at the hands of people who were still human.

Stella held all of the emotions down within her. She wouldn't let herself cry, wouldn't let a single tear slide down her cheeks. These monsters didn't deserve to see it. She wasn't going to give in. All Stella wanted to do right now was try to hold on to the sensation of living—these last moments of sheer existence. Just a little while longer, before it was gone.

"Yes, I'm certain that's my source. She has the blood," spoke a low voice that Stella recognized.

Stella looked up to see her contact, the nurse, whispering into the ears of administrators. She glared at him, but he refused to look at her. Maybe he could feel her eyes on him, but guilt kept his gaze away.

Why had she ever let herself trust him?

He seemed so normal. Nervous. Paranoid that the very walls had eyes that would turn on him at any moment. She had misjudged the man, never seeing him as a threat.

Word about her had spread among the nurses. There was always at least one person willing to trade with her. She hadn't worried that the information would fall into the wrong hands. The consequences for any kind of contact with a gang member were too severe for that.

Stella should have known something was off when he used an administrator key as a trade. How else would he have gotten it? They gave it to him, trying to lure her closer. It had all been too convenient, and she hadn't even noticed anything was wrong; she just let herself fall into the trap.

What little talking there was in the room ceased as a sharply dressed man with his hair gelled back joined her on the stage. The man clutched a microphone and walked around Stella with a smile, though she noticed he was careful never to come too close.

"Welcome one and all tonight!" he announced in the rich cadence of an announcer's voice.

"I'm Tristan Kotterman, your auctioneer, and what a lovely specimen we have here with us," Tristan said, gesturing at Stella without ever looking at her himself. "Gentlemen, just take a look here. Just take in the color of that skin. Might be the last time you ever get the chance." As he directed their attention, Stella felt the gazes of all of those eyes, now intensified, as they watched and speculated.

"Let's start the bidding at ten thousand pills. Do I hear ten thousand? Ten thousand, now eleven. Eleven thousand, will you give me twelve?"

Stella looked over the heads of the crowd as the numbers began to rattle off. She listened stoically as those numbers began to rise. How many people were "punished" in order for the administrators to hoard that many pills? How many people were killed under their system?

How bad did they want her? Why fight over her on the night that shipments failed to come? Now, when it seemed like they might actually need all of those extra pills. They were wasting them on her instead. She would never understand them.

She thought of Gavin again. Pictured him somewhere far away, somewhere safe, until the noise of the audience distracted her from her thoughts.

"Eight hundred thousand!" called out the administrator of entertainment, rising from his seat in excitement. It was hard to look at the man, with all those golden chains wrapped around his meaty neck and emerald rings encircling thick fingers.

"Eight hundred seventy thousand," countered the administrator of shipments coolly.

It had come down to the two most powerful men in the underground, men that were dressed in neat tailored suits, bidding for her with enough pills to supply over a hundred citizens for a full year. What would they do to her? Stella hoped that whatever it was, it would be over quick.

"Eight hundred seventy-four thousand," the entertainment administrator called out again, staring straight at Stella. She winced internally. She'd heard all the stories of what that man did to make his money. All those pretty girls vanishing, and how he had taken them away and let the guards use them.

What did he want with her?

"Now eight seventy-four, now eight seventy-four. Will you give me eight seventy-five? Now eight hundred seventy-four thousand. Eight hundred seventy-four thousand going once, going twice..."

"Nine hundred thousand," called out the administrator of shipments.

The entertainment administrator pounded his table in rage, and his personal guards shot to their feet to rush at the guards of the shipment administrator. Through the commotion, Stella began to feel weary as she watched them. Even if she closed her eyes, she wouldn't be able to shut out the image of all those great men, grown fat off their power. Men who were used to getting things their way and were quite unsure of what to do with themselves now that they had discovered that each one wanted the same thing.

Then a louder voice rang out, cutting across all the others like the roar of an angry bull. "ZERO PILLS."

The auction stopped as all heads careened around to the back of the room to see who had interrupted them. Stella looked too, squinting against the spotlight in her eyes to make out the owner of the voice. He leaned against the back wall, clutching the brick as if that slight hold was the only grip stopping him from launching himself into the crowd. It was the last person she had wanted to see here.

"Zero pills," Gavin repeated. "That is my offer—zero pills."

Stunned, Stella couldn't even bring herself to call out to him, couldn't warn him to run, to get away, back to his home. Now, when he still had the chance.

The shouting came again, all at once, as all the men in power tried to take charge simultaneously.

"Who do you think you are?"

"Get him out of here."

"You! Get that man! Bring him here."

A handful of guards rose uncertainly, attempting to follow conflicting orders. They all halted when they heard Gavin's next words.

"My name is Gavin Owings, son of Arthur Owings, the founder of the oxygen factory. I've disabled communications at the shipment station. If you don't let her go, none of you will ever get food or oxygen pills from the factory again."

Quiet murmurings from the crowd filled the room.

"Explain yourself," the administrator of entertainment demanded.

"I guess you didn't hear me the first time. The shipment station has been disabled, and your lives are at stake. Check it if you'd like," Gavin said.

"You can't do that," called out the administrator of entertainment.

"I already have," Gavin stated with an underlying power in each word that Stella had never heard from him before. "I'm one of the many men and women who work to get you the very pills you are using to sell this girl. I see that you've stockpiled pills, but it's not going to be enough. What you are doing here won't mean anything, because once you've run out of food, you are all going to die. It might take a week, or it might be months. But it will happen to all of you if you don't free her."

With that said, Gavin uncoiled himself from his place against the wall and walked toward the stage. His walk was met with a stiff silence as the men considered his words and did nothing. Out of habit, one advance guard, with his arms crossed over his chest, stepped in Gavin's path, blocking his progress.

Gavin glared at the guard and asked him a simple question. "Are you really going to try to stop me?"

Though he clenched his teeth and uncrossed his arms, the advance guard couldn't think of anything to say. He, too, stepped out of Gavin's way.

Stella's eyes fixed on Gavin as he walked up the stairs and joined her on the stage. Under her gaze, Gavin appeared self-conscious for the first time since he made his appearance in the administrators' lounge. He bowed his head as he reached for the rope binding Stella's hands and deftly untied it.

Once free, Stella reached for his rough hand and held it. As they walked out together, Stella marveled at the fact that in full sight of all the power of the underground, all the administrators and guards, Gavin had just strolled in and taken her away.

18

Gavin could still feel the cortisol flooding through his system. He could hear his blood pounding and his body still tense with the remnants of anger. He had never seen anything like that before: Stella bruised and tied up on a stage, and everyone bidding on her as if she weren't even human. Gavin didn't even want to think about how they had ended up with so many extra pills, after all of the hours he had poured into harvesting them. He knew that once he got back home, he had to do something about it.

The orders to leave the two of them alone had preceded them. Gavin found the route to the shipment station deserted. They had walked in silence, moving swiftly in case anything changed, back to the steel door that barred citizens from supplies that should have been distributed freely. If this was happening here, Gavin wondered for the first time, what was happening to the other settlements around the world? Were citizens receiving supplies elsewhere? Were the systems corrupted and flawed everywhere?

Gavin removed the brass key from his pocket and slipped it into the steel door, unlocking it. He pulled the door wide for Stella to walk through and then followed after her.

Caution forgotten, Stella walked around the shipment station, examining everything with wide eyes. She walked first to the dry dock, currently flooded behind four-inch polycarbonate Lexan, awaiting the arrival of the submarine from the oxygen factory, a submarine that hadn't arrived as scheduled for the first time in over fifteen years and would never arrive again without his access codes.

Her hands drifted across the chrome of the control center, with all of its buttons, its precise knobs and levers, now powered off and lifeless. Lastly, Stella came to a stop in front of a sleek glass screen before she turned around to face him. "What is it?"

"I'll show you." Gavin typed in the complex number sequence without having to think about it, as his fingers had memorized the codes long ago. He was immediately rewarded as the machine hummed to life, warming up, as he reactivated communications. Then the lights flashed on, first across the keyboard in the neon green colors of the factory, then illuminating the glass screen with the image of an empty desk.

"Hello?" Gavin called out. "Anyone there?" He heard light footsteps and caught a glimpse of tousled dark hair over a narrow face that stared blankly at him as if in disbelief without replying. Gavin didn't know if he was imagining it, but for a moment it looked like those short fingers hovered over the button marked "Cancel" before drifting away out of sight.

"Dad, he's on screen," the man called out before walking out of the line of the camera.

From behind him, Gavin felt the slender touch of fingers at his arm, and he turned to see Stella. Her eyes were fixed on the screen, and she wore a faint frown. "Gavin, who was that?" she whispered.

"My older brother, Morgan," Gavin explained. "He runs the shipments." Stella didn't say a word in reply. The touch of her fingers slipped away as Gavin once again heard the sound of footsteps hurrying over.

Even as an image on a screen, his father's presence was commanding. He was all masculine, with short-cropped hair and stubble on a crisp jaw line. The immaculate seams of his lab coat were stretched over solid muscles, and the badge reading "Arthur Owings, Founder and General Manager of Oxygen Factory" distinctly gleamed.

But as Gavin looked at his father's face, into gray eyes that were just like his own, he saw that they were marked with shadows that hadn't been there before. Gavin felt a twinge of guilt that he was the cause. This whole week had passed in a blur and Gavin had been caught up in it all, moment by moment. He had never even considered how everyone at his home would react to his disappearance.

Without wasting time, his father demanded, "Gavin, what happened? Where are you?"

"I'm in the underground city of the New Jersey region," Gavin said, answering the easy question first. He had to think quickly to decide how much of the story he wanted to tell.

"How did you end up there?" his father asked.

"I was hit in the back of the head when I was planting kelp. I lost consciousness and washed up on the shore," Gavin replied, just laying out the facts.

His father paused his questioning to process the details. "Do you have any idea who might have done it?"

"I'm not sure," Gavin stated, which wasn't entirely honest. His memory of what had happened was a blur. Yet, throughout the course of the week, he had begun to string different events together. Everything from what Sam had told him about the "nice man" who had given everyone in Celia's gang defective pills to all the hoarding abuse underground here... It all seemed to point to one person. Gavin just didn't want to say his suspicions yet. Not without evidence that it was true.

"Where have you been? You didn't get..." His father couldn't even say the words out loud. But the thought must have been torture. That his own son could have become contaminated out there and could be carrying the infection inside of him after all his work to stop that from happening.

"I'm fine, Dad. I've been on the pill. If one of the infected had gotten to me, that would be obvious, anyway," Gavin added.

"I'm sending the sub out for you, Gavin." As his father spoke, his long arms reached out for the control panel and sent out the instructions to do just that. His movements were stiff, with an almost lethargic touch, which made Gavin uneasy. "I couldn't even begin to tell you what's happened without you," he added.

He'd only been gone a week. What more could have gone wrong?

"Who's that behind you?" his father asked abruptly, suddenly realizing that Gavin wasn't alone. Gavin heard the command behind the words, telling him to get away. He couldn't mix. It wasn't safe.

Hearing herself mentioned, Stella strode forward in full sight of the screen, stopping right next to Gavin. His father's eyes widened when he took in her albino skin and violet eyes. Gavin knew that his father recognized Stella for what she was, just as he had. Albino specimens of nearly every species were immune to the toxins—humans included. "Where did you find her?"

"This is Stella. I didn't find her; she found me," Gavin said.

"Her blood could be the start of the cure," his father mused. "Or if that isn't possible, it could at least be the blueprint for inoculations."

There was something in the way his father stared at Stella, as if he were appraising her, that was too much like what Gavin had just seen. As if Stella was back on that stage, with administrators fighting over who got to kill her, or worse. Almost possessively, Gavin wrapped one arm around Stella and held her close. "She isn't some kind of experiment. She's a friend. I wouldn't have been able to make it here without her."

"I see." Arthur Owings leaned away from the screen and his gaze flickered from Gavin to Stella with interest. "But that isn't really up to you. That would be up to her. What would you say about it, Stella?"

For a moment, Stella was silent as she observed his father, considering his words. "What do you want from me?"

"All we would need is just a sample. Just a few drops of your blood should be enough," Arthur Owings said, folding his hands together under his chin as he waited for her reply.

"You think you can use my blood to stop the others from getting infected," Stella clarified, and Gavin wondered how that must make her feel. She had the opportunity to deny the people who had hunted her for years, who had just nearly killed her. Now Stella had the chance to get her revenge against the men who killed her father.

"All right," Stella said with a nod. "I'll do it."

"Gavin, would you do the honors?" his father asked him with satisfaction.

Gavin didn't have any other choice. He could feel his father's eyes on him as he dug through his bag of things from the factory and pulled out a syringe.

Stella held out her arm, palm upright. Gavin took care to disinfect the area around her wrist. As he brought the needle close to her vein, he paused. He didn't want to hurt her, not even this small bit. She had been hurt enough already.

"Don't worry, I'm used to it," she said. It was the amusement in her voice that finally snapped Gavin out of it. He gently pressed the needle into her vein and drew out the sample.

The glass filled red. As Gavin withdrew the needle from Stella, he found himself staring at its contents with interest. While he knew that Stella's skin was delicate enough for this sample to mark her with another bruise, the scientist in him was unabashedly curious.

He considered the implication of his father's words. Her blood could be a cure or an inoculation. Seeing firsthand the danger Stella went through by facing the infected, Gavin knew immunity didn't mean everything. The infected could kill whether someone had immunity or not. But immunity gave Stella something no other human had—she alone could breathe.

If his father was right, like he usually was, Stella's blood could be the start of something new. For the first time, they were on to something that could bring the world back to normal.

It was then that Gavin noticed the outside doors to the dry docks open with the entrance of the submarine. As all the water drained out and his way back home stood ready, Gavin had the sudden thought that it had never seemed to come so quickly. It was too soon.

"Gavin, I'll see you at the loading dock," Arthur ordered, only looking from the sample to see Gavin's nod in reply before the transmission went blank.

Gavin stared down at Stella, who was wrapped snugly into the crook of his arm. Looking at her now, Gavin could see all the bruises spread across her fair skin, a reminder that Stella wasn't all tough. She could be hurt out there so easily. He didn't want to think about just how vulnerable she really was. He didn't want to picture it, Stella walking back down all those hallways, facing the guards once again, and this time alone. He couldn't stand it.

"Come with me," Gavin said.

Stella looked up at him with wide eyes, and Gavin didn't know who was more surprised—him or her. The words were out of his mouth before he had time to even consider what he was asking. Gavin had just asked Stella to leave behind her entire life, everything and everyone she had ever known, to come with him, someone she had only known for a week. Yet, as Gavin waited for her answer with his heart pounding so hard he could hear it, he was glad he had said it.

"Would I never see the others again?" Stella asked, quietly.

"We have a transport submarine. You could take it out, and see them again." A trip would be easy enough to arrange—though it would be the perfect opportunity for his attacker to strike again.

"All right," Stella said. Despite all she had been through, there was a hint of a smile just at the corners of her mouth. "Let's go."

Carefully, deliberately, Gavin took Stella's hand and interlaced her fingers with his. Stella wasn't going to get hurt again. She wasn't going to get taken advantage of again, not even if it was his people at the oxygen factory who wanted to do it. He was going to protect her. Together, the two of them stepped into the submarine.

∼

THROUGH THE MURKY WATER, THERE WASN'T MUCH FOR THE two of them to see, save for the occasional school of fish. Infection had left the majority of life unchanged underwater, though Gavin did spot some deformed fish mixed in. One fish with three eyes and a crooked spine stood out among the others. Another had a body twice as long as its fellows and undulated in a wild pattern through the water.

Abruptly, Stella looked away from the school of fish. "I didn't want you to come after me, but I'm glad you did."

Gavin looked at the little he could see of her in the artificial glow of light. More than anything, her pale beauty in the darkness was unearthly, and it was easy to believe she was a spirit or an angel. Anything other than the real person who had helped him through all this. He wished he could know what she was thinking.

"Why didn't you want my help?" Gavin asked.

"I wanted you safe. I don't think I could live with myself if you died."

Gavin swallowed reflexively, trying not to get caught up in emotions, but to understand her instead. "Did you even think you were going to get past the guards?"

"There was a chance, even if it wasn't a good one," Stella admitted.

She had told him to go home, knowing that she'd probably end up dying. Dying for him.

"How could I go back to my old life never knowing if you made it out?" Gavin asked, shaking his head. It wouldn't have been right. Looking back, Gavin could see that this wasn't even the first time she had put herself in danger, and she had done it for him.

Gavin racked his brain, trying to filter through and explain emotions he had never experienced before. How could he let her know it wasn't fair? "Don't you know I feel the same way?"

A smile swept across Stella's features, wiping away the last traces of stress.

"I'm glad I'm here," Stella said, sliding closer to him. "After everything I did to get you home, I wouldn't want to lose you at the oxygen factory. Whoever attacked you isn't done. They're going to try it again."

Gavin didn't know what to say to that; he was too distracted by her presence. He couldn't take his eyes off her, from the curve of her cheek to the swell of her mouth. She was beautiful, and Gavin found himself leaning toward her, without making the conscious decision to do so. His lips found hers, met hers with a gentle pressure that sent heat down his spine and cleared out every thought from his mind.

"I think I love you," Stella whispered when they broke apart. "I've never felt that before." She sighed, resting her head down against his shoulder.

Gavin held her close to him and quietly marveled at the warmth of her, at her very presence here in his arms. "Sorry for repeating myself," Gavin replied when he finally got his thoughts collected, "but don't you know I feel the same way?"

He held her, watching their progress through the vast darkness of the ocean, until the moment when he could first see light piercing through the gloom. "Stella, look."

She picked up her head in time to see the dome jutting

up from the ocean floor. The dome was sky blue, lit from within its bionic membrane. When Gavin peered into the depths, he saw forms silhouetted within—all the different organisms that lived there, from the elephants to the albatross to the caracals and all the other life forms his father and the other scientists managed to save.

Stella watched, transfixed and wide-eyed the closer they got to the factory, as the sheer size of the place was revealed. The dome towered over them. What had started as a tiny underwater bunker had grown. First it had expanded with developments in technology; then, it grew with the world's need for it. Now, it stood the size of a city, illuminating the ocean floor.

As the submarine approached closer, Gavin could start to see all the biomes within the dome. From here, he could make out giraffes on the savannah, the binturongs and tigers of the forests, and the mixed herds of bison and cattle roaming through the prairie.

As they continued forward, Gavin could see his colleagues out in their green lab coats as they scurried about, gathering samples from their test subjects; as they picked fruits from the trees; as they walked about the biomes, clipboards in hand, recording data. Now that he could actually see the faces of the people he had known every day of his life, the realization hit him. They had done it. They had actually done it. He was home.

They slowed as the biomembrane recognized the submarine and folded around them, granting them access into the factory. Once inside, Gavin watched Stella's expression as the water drained away. Stella's hands trembled faintly. She bit her lip and folded her hands together. It was the first time he had seen her nervous.

Gavin tried to look at the factory again from Stella's

perspective. He knew Stella was well adapted for her life out among the infected. Though it was dangerous, Stella knew every component necessary to survive. She was lethal, and respected for it. All that she knew about the factory had come from his own experiences; he had left the factory with a near-fatal injury, without knowing the cause.

A small crowd gathered. Other scientists were running to their submarine, some still holding paperwork and test subjects. Among them, Gavin could see the tall profile of his father. Arthur Owings was not looking at him, but had his gaze locked on Stella.

Wordlessly, Gavin took Stella's hand and stood up with her. He paused with one hand on the doorframe and looked back at Stella. "Whatever happens, I'm here for you. I promise."

Stella pressed her palm tighter against his own, and the shadow of a smile lit up her face. "I know."

They walked into the factory together.

THANK YOU FOR READING!

If you enjoyed reading, please leave a review! Honest reviews help bring the book to the attention of other readers.

ABOUT THE AUTHOR

Renée des Lauriers is the author of the Breathless series.
Renée was raised by a folk-singer and an accountant to be
analytically creative. From thirteen, she played guitar and
sang on stage at coffee shops. She also oil painted and wrote
poetry on odd paper scraps. Besides writing, Renée has
worked as an emergency medical technician and a high
school English teacher. Now she lives in California with her
family. Visit Renée online at www.reneedeslauriers.com.